LAST MISTAKE

LAUREN BIEL

Copyright © 2023 by Lauren Biel

All rights reserved.

No part of this book may be reproduced in any form or by any electronic or mechanical means, including information storage and retrieval systems, without written permission from the author, except for the use of brief quotations in a book review.

This is a work of fiction. Names, characters, events, and incidents are the products of the author's imagination. Any resemblance to actual persons, living or dead, or actual events is purely coincidental.

Library of Congress Cataloging-in-Publication Data

Last Mistake/Lauren Biel 1st ed.

Cover Design: Lori Rivera

Editing: Anna @ Corbeaux Editorial Services

Proofreading: Sugar Free Editing

Interior Design: Sugar Free Editing

For more information on this book and the author, visit: www.LaurenBiel.com

Please visit LaurenBiel.com for a full list of content warnings.

For those of us who dream of being pursued by a masked stranger

CHAPTER 1

Mason

Moans beneath me fueled my thrusts. I gripped her hair in my fist as I took her in secret—the best kind of sex. The gentle sound of a door creaking open reached me from across the room, and my stomach sank. It wasn't my parents... which meant it was—

My gaze shot toward the cracked-open door, and what I'd tried to avoid stared back at me.

"Mason?" the blonde beneath me said as my hips stalled. "What the hell is the matter?"

The girl in the doorway—Harley—narrowed her eyes, and I threw a hand over her best friend's mouth. Guilt stabbed a double-edged sword beneath my ribs. As much as I liked to mess with Harley, I had fucked up this time. I had *royally* fucked up.

The woman beneath me ripped my hand away and sat up on her elbows. Her messy blonde locks draped over her shoulders as she looked toward the door. "What the fuck?" she snapped.

I climbed off her, half tugging my pants up as my feet hit the floor. "Harley just saw us," I said with a long exhale.

"Wait, what?" Anna looked at me, her jaw slack. "You said she wouldn't be home!"

"She wasn't supposed to be," I said as I zipped up my jeans and left the half-naked girl on my bed. I left the room to search for Harley, even knowing she would be beyond pissed. Deservedly so. "Harley?" I called out, but there was no response.

By the time I found her, she had made it across the house to the screened-in porch. Her dark hair draped over her shoulder as she leaned on her fist. She was staring into the evergreens, her favorite—and the most boring—of the trees surrounding our house.

"Don't," she said, lifting her hand to stop me before I could speak.

"Harley..."

"She's my best friend, Mason. The only person I trust. Well, *trusted*, past tense, thanks to you."

"Why do you care so much? How does it even affect you if me and Anna have a casual thing?"

"First off, Anna doesn't do anything *casually*. Secondly, you're—"

"What, Harley? Say it. Not good enough for your friend?"

"Of course you aren't! You're not a good person. Must we rehash why?"

Ouch. But fair. I had a teensy-weensy little sexual assault charge that came from a dumb night with friends. They'd drugged a girl, and while I hadn't partaken in the act, I also hadn't made any effort to stop it. I spent a few months in juvie because of it, but Harley felt I deserved a steeper punishment.

"I didn't do anything to that girl, Hal."

"That's what you say." She shook her head. "I told you to stay away from my friends. It's the *one* thing I've asked you to do. You've made my life hell since we were kids, Mason. *Hell.*"

She was right about that. I'd spent my life torturing Harley since we were kids. I hated that my mother had married her father. He swept my mom off her feet like she needed to be rescued, even though everything bad that ever happened to us was because of her and her drinking problem. A decade didn't make a difference. He transformed my mother into some princess, but under that, the woman who lived in a run-down home remained, drinking away her problems and ignoring mine.

I was the one who needed rescuing most of the time, not her, but Harley's dad couldn't buy my love like he had my mom's. Nine-year-old me disliked him then as much as nineteen-year-old me did now.

"I didn't do this to you on purpose, if that's what you're implying." I stepped toward her, and she scooted her chair farther away. She looked at me, and hatred accompanied the disgust she felt for me before I ever slept with her friend. "Maybe I like her, Harley."

Her blue-gray eyes shot up. "Do you?"

My gaze fell the moment hers met mine. "Ish."

"Jesus Christ. This is what I mean! You do things just to spite me!" She rose to her feet and went to push past me. I stopped her with a step to the side. She burned me with her anger, engulfed in her distaste for me, and I couldn't help but smirk when she pouted her lips like she did when we were kids before she ran off to tattle on me. She knew better than to do that, though. I had already caused enough trouble for her fucking daddy.

She raised her chest, trying to look tougher, but that only drew my attention to her cleavage. I didn't stare long, because unlike Anna, Harley wasn't even eighteen yet. Just shy of it. Her posturing didn't intimidate me. I was bigger than her, no matter how much she puffed her chest. She had no chance in this fight.

It was a stalemate. Neither of us moved.

"Hal..." I whispered, trying to calm her down.

"Fuck you!" Her frustration boiled over, and she burned her way past me with heavy steps.

Something told me she would never forgive me for sleeping with her friend. Well, I haven't forgiven her father for sleeping with my mother either. We're closer to even.

CHAPTER 2

Harley

Fuck him. Mason was the single most selfish person on the planet. He did nothing that didn't benefit him or hurt me. Ever since my father started dating his mom, he'd taken out his frustration on me. *I* wasn't the one dating her.

I sat down on the bed with a groan and stared up at the glitter-painted ceiling. When I was younger, I thought it was the best idea, but much like having a stepbrother, it ended up being uglier each year that passed.

My cat stood up with a stretch and sauntered over to me. I rubbed his fluffy orange cheek. "Sammy," I cooed. He always knew when I was upset.

Mason and his mother were allergic to cats, so he mostly stayed in my room, but it was big enough for a king like him. He curled up beside me, his weight pressing into my leg.

I couldn't stop replaying what I'd seen. His shaggy blond hair in the crook of her neck as he fucked her. The waves of her lighter blonde hair falling off the edge of the bed. His jeans half down his ass because he'd been too rushed to even take them off. His intense green eyes meeting mine before I hightailed it out of there. I'd imagined that sweet blonde girl who got assaulted at the party two years ago beneath him, and a shiver had raked my spine. Hearing Anna's voice instead ripped me from that thought and thrust me into something worse—the reality that he was screwing my best friend. The betrayal was too much to handle.

A tear fell down my cheek.

He'd only had sex with Anna so that he could rip away the one person who mattered most to me. My best friend. He didn't *like* her. Mason didn't like anyone.

A knock sounded on the bedroom door. I lifted my gaze and wiped the tears from my cheeks. I hated crying, but I couldn't help it. I was so damn frustrated. Before I could welcome whomever it was inside—or turn them away—the door creaked open, and Anna appeared in the doorway. She had a lot of nerve.

"Harley . . ." she whispered. She looked fucked. Her T-shirt was even on backward.

I scoffed.

"Please, don't be mad at me."

"How could you do that to me, Anna?"

She brushed her hair behind her ears, a nervous habit she had. "I didn't do it *to* you. I did it for me."

I blew out an exhale that lifted my auburn hair off my forehead. "Do you think he *loves* you, Anna? Mason has never loved anything in his fucking life."

Anna's cheeks flushed red, then the color clawed down her chest. "You're just jealous."

My eyes leaped to hers. "Are you serious? What am I jealous about?"

Anna's hands planted on her hips. "Well . . . you just

don't want me to find someone and be happy. If I have a boyfriend, you'll be alone."

"You can get a boyfriend, Anna. Have as many as you want. I don't care! But why does it have to be *him*?"

Anyone but him. Mason assaulted that girl. I knew it in my gut. He wasn't this sweet, demure man who would sit idly by instead of speaking up. No, Mason was confident and didn't think about anyone but himself. Even if he didn't partake, he probably still enjoyed watching. Mason Sheridan was a bad person, and he didn't deserve someone like Anna.

"Why do you hate him so much?" Anna asked, her voice softening as she approached.

I considered telling her the truth. It was the only way to get her to understand why I was this upset. No one understood why I felt the way I did because Mason's records had been sealed as a youth. I decided to spill Mason's guts. "Mason was seventeen and best friends with this guy who was like twenty-one. Jeff Barnes."

Anna's head cocked. "The dude who drugged that girl?"

"Yeah, that one. Only Jeff hadn't acted alone." My fingers fiddled with the weighted blanket on my bed, tracing the threads that held the beads within the intricate design.

Her eyes widened. "No . . . Harley, he wouldn't—"

"You don't know him. Hell, I hardly know him, and I've spent most of my life beside him. He was there, Anna."

She shook her head. "He never got in trouble."

I scoffed. "Yes, he did. Lucky for him, my father had good lawyers. Pleaded him down as far as they could, but he still went to juvie for it."

Anna sat down beside me and dropped her head into her hands. "I had no idea."

"Will you stop seeing him?" I asked. I wasn't sure what

I'd do if she said no. I wasn't sure I could be friends with her while knowing she was sleeping with him. Part of me knew she wouldn't be able to stay with him, though, because of her past. She'd been drugged and assaulted before, though she remembered very little, and nothing happened to the guy who'd raped her. If Mason did do it, and he walked free, he'd be the embodiment of what was done to her too.

"Men are such fucking liars." Tears welled in her eyes, and I couldn't help but sit up and wrap my arms around her. "I thought he liked me," she whined through sobs.

"Mason doesn't like anyone but himself."

CHAPTER 3

Mason

I raised my phone and sent another text.

> Hey. Again.

The third text to Anna changed to *read* status, and I put the phone down on the table beside my bed. She probably chose her friendship over what we had. *What'd we really even have? A few good nights of sex?* I tried to rationalize with myself. My phone pinged, and I picked it up and looked at it.

> Rapist

That was the last text I got before she blocked me. I kept staring at the word. *Rapist*. I was not, but I knew who fucking thought I was.

I got out of bed and walked toward the kitchen. There was no one around, and not a single clink of sound reached my ears. I went to her bedroom but found it empty. The more rooms I checked, the more the anger rose and boiled my blood. Harley had *no* right to spew lies like that. It wasn't a story for her to tell.

By the time I found her in the library, tugging a book off the shelf, the anger within me was a fire that lapped at my insides. I grabbed her and shoved her against the shelves. The books rattled behind her, and she dropped the book she'd been taking off the shelf, a pained wince crossing the features of her face.

"Why?" I snapped, shaking her and causing a whimper to leave her parted lips. I tried to control the anger leaching out of my fingertips, because as mad as she made me, I didn't want to hurt her.

Her back arched to keep the hard wooden shelf from stabbing into her. Her eyes widened. "What?" she asked, her voice straining beneath my weight.

"Why did you tell Anna I raped that girl?" The words came from deep within me and blurred my vision on the way out. I thought seeing red was just a saying, but I was that angry. "I have never raped anyone, Harley. How many times do I have to tell you that? You were at the trial. You saw that I was innocent." My gaze dropped before lifting back to hers.

She scoffed, and it made me want to strangle her to stop that sound leaving her mouth. "You aren't innocent."

Not wholly. I knew that.

"Innocent of *that*." I shook my head. "I never raped that girl."

Heat crept behind my eyes, and I fought the threat of a tear that tried to surface. What I saw was bad, I'd admit that, but I didn't touch her. I'd be forever plagued by my silence. She'd never understand that, because she never cared to let me explain. The moment the police officer came and carted me to the station, she'd solidified her belief about what happened, and nothing I could say would change that.

She saw me as the wild and crazy older brother who'd always done petty shit to annoy her. I was the troublemaker who'd gotten the underside of his dick pierced in secret when he was seventeen. I was the delinquent who'd learned how many liquor bottles he could stuff inside his pants at the local store without getting caught. I was the idiot who hung out with some unsavory people. These things did *not* mean I'd assaulted anyone, though. I was a bit of a rebel, not a fucking rapist.

But none of what I said would matter. In her eyes, I was the sinner and she was the saint.

"I don't believe you, Mason," she snarled.

"I don't need you to. The jury of my fucking peers did. And most importantly, the person who actually did it is behind bars." I inhaled deeply before exhaling. "But you can't be the new judge, jury, and executioner. That's not fair."

Her haunting gray eyes stared at me. They narrowed and her lower jaw jutted out. "I will be whatever I need to be to protect my friend from you."

"There's nothing I can do to get you to believe me, is there?" I asked through gritted teeth.

She shook her head, her gaze not wavering as those accusatory eyes bore through me.

I released her, picked up her book, and handed it to her. "Stay out of my life," I said as I walked away.

She drove me to needing a drink. To numb the white-hot anger burning me from the inside out. I slammed the library door and went back to the kitchen. The lights blinded me as I stepped into them. The midday sunrays assaulted the overhead skylight, piercing the glass and landing on the granite island below. I walked around the colorful glow of light on the tiled floors to get to where they kept the liquor. The minifridge blended in with the rest of the fancy wooden cabinets and produced a low hum—the only clue as to the whereabouts of the booze stash hidden behind the wood. I opened it, grabbed her daddy's favorite whiskey, and removed the cap. After downing several large gulps, I replaced the cap and melted the red wax around it with a Zippo from my pocket. They'd be none the wiser now.

I returned to my room, my body feeling the same hum as that refrigerator. Warmth radiated through me and flushed my skin. It'd been a while since I drank. I'd stayed away from alcohol since the party, where things got much too out of control.

I sat down on the bed, the silk sheets reminding me of just how different everything was from my life before the Taylors. I'd take the ripped, cheap cotton over this luxury life I never fit into any day. Unlike my mother, I couldn't be twisted and turned until I fit into the round hole Harley's father tried to cram me into.

When I opened my drawer, I looked at the necklace I'd bought for Harley for her upcoming eighteenth birthday. It had a pair of evergreen trees on a rustic metal background. It was pretty, or so I thought, and I hated evergreens. Without a second glance, I tossed it into the garbage beside my bed. She wouldn't get shit from me since she couldn't stand to share the same air with a horrid monster like me.

I was misguided, not a monster, but it was hard to change the mind of someone who saw you in their nightmares.

CHAPTER 4
TWO YEARS LATER

Harley

College life hadn't been what I'd expected. I excelled in high school and hardly had to crack open a textbook to keep myself on top. I didn't expect college to be *this* much harder. That miscalculation dropped my GPA lower than I wanted for my freshman year. I was dedicated to getting that 4.0 this year though, and that meant having my nose in a book as often as I humanly could. At least if I was going to be stuck at home studying, it wasn't in a dorm. My dad rented a quaint two-bedroom house with a beautiful wall of windows overlooking a heated pool. All for me.

I looked away from the blurring words on the pages beneath me and stared at the steam rolling off the surface of the pool. The water called to me. There was nothing like a nighttime swim beneath the moonlight to de-stress.

I went and changed into my bathing suit. It was nothing fancy, just a black one-piece that still made me feel too bare. I opened the sliding-glass door and stepped onto the patio. The cold air wrapped around me, reminding me that it was

October and soon the whole area would be covered in snow. Lights dotted the in-ground pool's perimeter, and the moon reflected off the surface of the water. It lit up so much of the backyard, I almost forgot it was nine at night. I set my towel on a nearby chair and jumped into the water. Eighty-five degrees never felt so good as the warmth embraced me. I broke through the surface and ran my hands through my dark, wet hair. A branch snapping drew my attention, and I spat water as I looked around. Aside from the water rippling around me, the backyard lay still.

"Hello?" I called out, wiping a hand down my face. Silence answered me. I couldn't shake the eerie feeling that I was being watched, and it sucked the joy out of the relaxing nighttime swim. I swam toward the ladder and climbed out, wrapping the towel around me and taking one quick glance over my shoulder before going inside and locking the door.

Even once inside and locked away, I couldn't shake the uncomfortable feeling surrounding me.

Mason

I wasn't watching Harley because I liked her. Quite the contrary. Our last interactions had been pretty negative, and I'd moved out soon after and gotten my own apartment. Even though she thought I was terrible, she needed to be watched because there were truly worse people out there. People who actually did what she thought I'd done. Jeff Barnes was one of the monsters she needed to fear.

I'd testified against him, not to save my own ass but because I genuinely hated what I'd witnessed. He was supposed to get just under six years in jail, but he got out at four for good behavior. I scoffed because the good behavior in prison was only so he could get out and get back to the bad behavior. He'd promised me he'd get back at me. What was it he'd said?

"Your little sister? She's going to be awake when I show her what it's like to be ripped apart from the inside out."

The moment I found out he was being released, I began to tail Harley. It was easy. She didn't really do anything when she wasn't in class besides stay at home and study. Sometimes she took a swim, like tonight. Most nights, I just made sure no one crept around like I was. Usually I stayed in the car, but tonight I got closer, walking along the trees and listening to see if anyone else was around. When I'd stepped on that branch, my stomach had climbed into my throat. If she caught me, I could only imagine the sweet hell I'd hear from her. She'd call me a creep, which I kind of deserved, or she'd worry I was there to assault her.

When I went back to the car, I released a sigh of relief because she hadn't spotted me. Even if she heard me out and believed I was watching her for her own good, she would then live in fear, and I knew how hard she was working toward her goal this year in school. I wished Harley realized she didn't need to waste so much of herself on college. There was more to life than killing yourself over a degree. College was never really for me. Or maybe I wasn't meant for college. Either way, I never bothered going. Instead, I got a welding license, and I was damn good at my job.

Satisfied she was safe for the night, I drove away and headed toward my apartment. I was exhausted by the time I pulled into the parking lot, and I made it inside with just enough energy to have a quick smoke before nearly crawling to my bed. I kept watch over Harley most of my time outside of work, which left no time to do much of anything else, and exhaustion became my constant state. I wouldn't be able to keep this schedule up for long, not without risking my job.

Six a.m. came way too quickly every single morning. My eyelids felt like lead curtains as I rolled over to turn off my alarm. Every day I wondered why I was doing all this for her. Why I was killing myself just to make sure she didn't get hurt by the very person she thought I was like.

I climbed out of bed and got right into the shower. I leaned my forehead against the ceramic wall and let the cold water run over me, trying to wake myself up. I ran on cold showers, coffee, and cigarettes these days. Once I dressed, I grabbed a breakfast bar to eat on the go and headed out the door. I always checked Harley's locks first thing in the morning, long before she'd woken up to go to class, to make sure the front door and the sliding-glass door were still locked.

Everything was locked and quiet at her house. She was safe for another night. And I was having a bad fucking time making sure of that.

CHAPTER 5

Harley

I gave in and admitted I needed help with calculus. Nothing even seemed to be in English, and I found myself rereading questions half a dozen times and still not knowing what I was being asked to solve. I sat across from Ellie, a junior calculus extraordinaire. Even with her translating, I still couldn't get it. When would I ever measure the area of a curve?

"You might as well change to an online course and pay me to do it for you at this rate," she said as she put down her pencil.

"I'm not giving up yet," I told her. I wasn't ready to throw in the towel.

"Suit yourself." She gathered her books and flashed her dark brown eyes at me. They contrasted her near-white hair.

"Are you leaving? We hardly—"

"I have to get ready for a party tonight."

I cocked my head and stood up. "What kind of party?"

"For Halloween," she said, tucking her books beneath her arm.

"A little early, eh?"

"It's Halloween every Friday in October, Harley." We stared at each other in awkward silence. "Did you want to come?" she finally asked.

I hadn't realized I was waiting for an invite. I never went to parties, but I wouldn't have minded forgetting about the area of a fucking curve for a night. I nodded with a hint of overexcitement.

"Do you even have a costume?" she asked as her hand dropped to her hip. She didn't actually want me to go, but I'd made no friends since I started college. If I was going to be a failure, at least I wouldn't have to be so lonely.

I thought for a moment. "I'll figure something out. What's the address?"

Ellie wrote down the address and gave me a half hug before she hurried out the door. "See you tonight."

The moment I closed the door, I tried to compile some kind of Halloween costume from what I had at the house. I grabbed a pair of knee-high boots, black shorts, a sequined shirt, and an old masquerade mask that was part of my birthday party outfit last year. I wasn't anything in particular, but it would do.

I got dressed, smoothing the wrinkles from my shirt. The mask was pulled up on my forehead as I did my makeup. Dark eyeliner encased my eyes, and mascara extended every lash. Once I was finished, I grabbed the address, plugged it into my phone, and took an Uber to the party.

The drive was short, and the off-campus house was a bigger version of the house I lived in. Cars lined both sides of the street, and I was glad I'd taken a rideshare when I realized there wouldn't have been anywhere to park if I'd taken my own car.

When I walked in, I knew that it was more of a junior- and senior-level party. Everyone looked so much older than me, but I'd always been baby-faced. I was fairly certain I wouldn't be the youngest student at the party, but it was now clear I hovered somewhere near the bottom. I held my sweater against me as I looked around. Loud, disorienting music pounded through every pore. Costumes varied from sexy and slutty to dark and scary. The scents of sweat and beer mingled as I moved through the crowd and searched for Ellie.

A man wearing a black shirt, black pants, and a devil mask stared at me so hard that it made my cheeks flush. I couldn't see anything but the skin of his neck and hands. He kicked off the wall and walked over to me.

"What's your name?" he asked.

"Harley!" I yelled over the music.

"Pretty name," he said as he leaned his shoulder into me. "I'm Ian. Let me get you a drink." His hand grazed my waist as he stepped away.

I stood in the center of the mass of bodies, awaiting his return as the rest of the room danced around me. He came back, shimmying through people to get to me. He placed a red Solo cup in my hand, and I stared at the dark liquid sloshing inside. I took a sip and it burned my throat on the way down. The masked devil turned me around, and we started dancing, slow and sensual. The liquor buzzed through me even though I'd only taken a couple of sips. Someone knocked into me and spilled the rest of my cup all over me and the floor. *Fuck.* Ian cursed behind me, more upset than I was, and I was the one who got covered in liquor.

"God damn it," he said with a hollow masked sound. "I'll get you another one."

Ian left me alone in the middle of the living room, and I felt that shiver of someone watching me again. Even through the buzz in my body, I tightened up on myself as my eyes scanned the crowd. Something felt wrong. My eyes fell on a tall man in one of those scary Purge masks, with big purple X's for eyes and a grotesque smile. I couldn't take my eyes off him. He looked so out of place in his hoodie and jeans.

Mason

I HADN'T BEEN TO A PARTY LIKE THIS SINCE *THE INCIDENT*. Nothing good came from them. I never expected Harley to go to one of these. I was just about to leave when I saw her get into a car that wasn't familiar to me, dressed up like that, and I had to follow her. I had an LED Purge mask in my trunk in case I ever needed to hide my identity from her. I just hadn't thought I'd ever need it. I parked down the road, opened my trunk, and took on the identity in my hands.

When I walked into the party, panic cut off my breath for a moment. There were a lot of similarities between the two parties, even though they'd occurred over four years apart. Pushing past that claustrophobic feeling, my gaze darted around. I had to at least get Harley in my sights. My stomach sank when I saw her and recognized the mask of the man behind her. The signature hand-drawn eyebrows told me exactly who it was.

I squeezed closer to her by blending in with the crowd. When I was close enough, I knocked into the girl beside her, and Harley's drink spilled down her shirt. I felt bad about it, but I knew what was in that drink. I backed away until I was against the wall, just watching her. I knew he'd be back with another drink, and I'd have to figure out some way to get it away from her without being noticed.

I tucked my hands into my pockets and tried to look as unapproachable as I could when her attention fell on me. He came back and handed another drink to her, and she took a small sip. I walked over, danced a little, and "accidentally" knocked into her, spilling her cup all over me and the damn floor. Curse words flew from behind her.

"What the fuck, man?" he yelled as he stepped toward me. I towered over him and didn't back down.

"It was an accident," I said, lowering the tone of my voice so she wouldn't recognize it.

"Accident my ass," he said before drawing his arm back to punch me. I stepped aside, and he ended up falling into a group of girls. Their men squared up to him, and I ushered Harley away from the fray.

"Why do I feel like that wasn't an accident?" she said as her eyes rolled up to meet mine. I thought for a second that she might've recognized me, but she leaned her body into mine. She'd never do that to Mason. With glassy eyes, she took an unsteady step.

"Come on, you're drunk," I said as I reached for her arm.

She tugged out of my grasp, her lip pouting out. "I don't want to leave yet," she whined.

If I pushed her out the front door, it would cause a scene. I looked down the hallway. Ties and socks dangled from doorknobs. I knew what that meant. One door at the end of the hall remained devoid of decoration, and I begrudgingly guided her toward it. She leaned into me for support.

"I'm Harley," she slurred.

I thought for a moment, not having planned an alter ego tonight, despite the mask. "I'm Guy," I whispered. Not creative, but all I could think of at the time.

She giggled. "That's not your real name."

"Family name," I told her as I ushered her toward the door. I brought her into the room, looked around to make sure it was empty, and closed the door behind us. I twisted the lock, and she tumbled onto the bed with a laugh. I rolled my eyes. I wasn't in the mood to babysit her.

"Come," she whined, motioning me closer with her hand.

I shook my head.

"Please!"

I gave in and climbed into bed with her. She pressed her body against me as her head lolled to the side. I knew what that piece of shit gave her, and I knew she wouldn't remember this tomorrow.

Just when I thought she was out, she turned toward me. "Let me see your face!" She pawed at my mask, and I grabbed her wrists.

No way. "Leave it on," I told her.

When she pouted dramatically, I quieted her by drawing her closer and turning her onto her side. She nestled against me, and I knew she'd fall right asleep. The heat of her made me hard, so I turned my lap away from her warmth. Guilt tightened my belly when I realized my sister was in bed with me and that I got fucking hard, even if it wasn't on purpose. I shuddered at the thought of what would've happened to her if I hadn't been there. Jeff would've made good on his promise. He'd have ripped her apart. As much as Harley hated me, she needed me. It was all my fault in the first place, but I was the only one who could protect her.

Soft snores came from her, and knowing she was safe with me for the night, I let myself fall asleep as well.

CHAPTER 6

Harley

I woke up in bed with a masked man. My tongue felt like sandpaper, and my head felt like it was in a vise. I didn't recall drinking that much, but I couldn't remember anything after my drink spilled on me. My shorts were still on, which was a good sign. Even my boots were still zipped up to my knees. I looked at the man beside me. He was tall, underdressed, and wearing a Purge mask. He stirred awake.

"Oh, good morning," he said in a deep and gravelly voice.

"Where are we?" I asked, though it felt like my tongue stuck to the roof of my mouth with every syllable.

"A Halloween party," he said as he slipped his arm from behind my head and stood up. "What time is it?" he asked.

I checked my watch. "Eight a.m."

"Shit, I'm going to be late for work," he said as he went for the door. He stopped and looked back at me. "Can I bring you home?"

"If you're already late, I'll just call a ride."

"No!" he said, much too loudly. "I would like to see you home myself."

I considered telling him no, but he sounded desperate. "Fine," I said. "How much did I drink?"

"A lot." He handed my sweater to me, and we stepped into the dim hallway. Discarded cups and clothes speckled the floor. Sleeping people lay on random surfaces throughout the house. It was a mess. I looked around for the man with the devil mask, but he was gone.

The guy wearing the Purge mask brought me to his car. It looked and smelled brand new. "I'm covered in spilled liquor," I said, gesturing to his perfect leather seats.

"Doesn't matter, just get in," he said.

I raised my mask to my forehead and looked in the mirror. Smeared makeup stained my cheeks. "You can take your mask off," I said to him.

"I look like shit. I'll take it off when I'm alone."

I shrugged, and he put the car in drive and started toward my house. "Don't you need my address?" I asked.

"Oh yeah, sorry. I was just driving toward more off-campus housing."

I gave him my address, and we bumped along the road in silence. He pulled into my driveway and grabbed my arm when I went to get out. "Are you going again next Friday?" he asked.

I shrugged. "Maybe. Are you going?"

"Maybe."

"See you next week, maybe," I said with a smile. I got out of the car, closed the door, and knocked on the window. He lowered it, and I leaned down to look at his masked face. "Thanks for not sleeping with me."

"N-no problem," he stammered, as if it was a weird thing to say thank you for, but it meant a lot to me. With everything that'd happened with fucking Mason, I was glad I'd ended up falling asleep with someone who had self-control. Chivalry didn't have to be dead.

Mason

I THREW THE SWEATY MASK OFF THE MOMENT I GOT TO THE end of her street. It was actually one of the best nights of sleep I'd had since Jeff got out of jail. I knew she was safe because she was with me. But Harley would never be around me willingly. If she went to the party next week, I'd have to go along behind her and keep my eyes on her all over again. It'd take everything in me not to kill Jeff if he came to the next party.

No, it wasn't *if*. It was *when*. Those parties were his feeding grounds, and I hadn't been surprised to see him there. He'd be starving by now, and Harley was on the menu.

I grabbed a quick breakfast on the way to work and went in wearing the same clothes from last night. The scent of liquor clung to my outfit, and I knew my boss smelled it the moment I came in. He shook his head, and I knew I'd hear about it later. But what choice did I have? I had to keep an eye on Harley because if anything happened to her, it would be all my fault.

I gathered my tools and went to my station.

"Mason! Can I see you for a minute?" boomed the voice from the office.

I lowered my tools and walked into the barren office. "Yeah, what's up?"

"That's what I'd like to know. You haven't been yourself for the last week," my boss said as he leaned forward at his desk.

"I'm dealing with some family stuff, and I'm struggling to keep up with everything."

He took a deep breath. "Mason, you're such a good welder. Dare I say one of our best guys? I don't want to lose you. What if you took a week off and handled whatever it is that you're dealing with? I'd rather you do that than come in smelling like a bar floor."

I shook my head. "That's not necessary."

"It's not really a suggestion. You have to take the week off. It's better than an official suspension."

I sighed. "Thank you, Mr. Elliott."

I left the office, filled with annoyance and relief. At least it gave me some time to figure shit out.

I went home, took a well-earned shower, and got dressed. I packed a bag and looked back at my apartment before flipping off the lights. I'd be back, possibly quicker than I thought. I needed to stay with Harley to keep her safe. Jeff knew she was a student now, and it wouldn't take him long to find out where she lived.

The drive to Harley's house was so familiar that I could do it in my sleep. Some nights, I almost did. Instead of parking in her driveway, I parked in a lot down the road. I couldn't allow her to see me in the car I took her home in this morning.

I slung my backpack over my shoulder and walked to her house. I took the familiar steps to her door, checked the knob out of instinct, and then knocked. Harley opened the door, looking tired and worn down. She would never be the party-girl type.

Her eyes narrowed when she saw me. "What are you doing here?"

"Can I stay with you for a little while? A few weeks, a month max."

She couldn't shake her head fast enough. "Absolutely not. What's wrong with your apartment?"

"They're remodeling the units on my floor."

"Home?"

"Too far from work. My car is in the shop for repairs."

"Convenient," she said as she tried to close the door in my face.

"Hal, for fuck's sake. I'll owe you one." I exhaled. "Please." I didn't mean to sound so desperate, but I needed her to let me stay. For my own sanity. I couldn't keep going like this, making late-night and early-morning trips.

She rolled her eyes. "I'll add it to the pile of IOUs from you over the years." She scoffed before stepping aside and letting me in. Her gaze burned me. "Just until your apartment is done, and then you have to go, Mason. I'm not kidding. The second it's finished."

Yeah, I'd be gone when I knew she was safe. When I'd taken a couple weeks after my break from work to get back in my boss's good graces. She'd just have to deal with it. Neither of us wanted me to be there.

CHAPTER 7

Harley

I thought I'd gotten away from Mason. I'd hardly spoken a sentence to him since he moved out two years ago, before I started college. I didn't even think he knew my address. Mason only came around when he needed things, and this time was no different.

I turned to him. "Don't bother me when I'm studying, which means pretty much don't bother me at all." I gestured down the hall. "You can use the spare bedroom."

He didn't speak to me as he went down the hall and made himself right at home. I wished I could've brought my cat, because at least if Mason was going to be here to bother me, he'd suffer too.

I grabbed my books and went to the couch. I plopped down, flipped open the first book, and started studying. I kept looking back at the hall that led to the spare bedroom, already too distracted by his presence. I couldn't help but wonder what he was doing and what he'd been up to for two freaking years. I sat back with a huff and tried to focus on the words in front of me. Just as I got into the studying bubble, he walked out in nothing but swim shorts. My eyes rolled up his body before annoyance snapped my gaze away.

"What are you doing?" I asked, slamming my book closed.

"Going for a swim?" he said with a cock of his head. "Are there pool hours I need to know about?" He raised one stupid eyebrow at me.

God. He was such a nuisance. "No, I guess not." I shook my head. "Don't you have work or something to go to?"

"I have the week off," he said, throwing a towel over his broad shoulder.

I scoffed. "Of course you do."

"So hostile, Hal." He smirked, opened the sliding-glass door, and stepped onto the deck, staring at me as he eased the door closed until only a small crack remained. "You can join me if you want."

"Not a chance in hell."

He didn't say anything as he closed the door the rest of the way. I watched through the window as he put his towel on a chair and dove into the pool. He popped back up, threw his head back, and wiped a hand through his golden-blond hair. When he turned around and looked at me, a smirk on his face, I dropped my gaze back to my book and hoped he didn't notice.

Mason

I SHOULDN'T HAVE COME TO HER HOUSE AND GONE RIGHT TO annoying her, but it was so damn easy. I liked the red hue which sprang to her cheeks and how her jaw tensed so hard it made her lower lip tremble. It was cute.

When I turned around and saw her staring, I couldn't help but smile at her. She remained glued to her book as I climbed out of the pool and grabbed my towel to dry off. The cool fall air made my skin pebble with goosebumps. I was half-tempted to jump back into the pool just to escape the cold. Instead, I went inside.

It was so chilly in the house, and I swore it was from the ice queen on the couch in the living room. I went over to the thermostat and changed it from sixty-five to seventy-five.

"Uh, excuse me? What are you doing?" she asked.

"Turning the heat up. You may like being frigid, but I don't," I said as I rubbed the towel through my hair.

"You can't come in here and be a fucking pest," she snapped.

"Don't get your panties in a bunch, Harley. How about seventy? That seems like a good compromise."

"Don't talk about my panties," she said under her breath, but not low enough.

I walked past her and rubbed a hand through her hair as if she were a child. She smacked my hand away and nearly growled. I left her in the living room, a flurry of curse words following me all the way to my new bedroom. Once I'd dressed and returned to the living room, Harley proceeded to actively ignore me. I walked into the kitchen and started clanging cupboard doors as I looked for something to make for lunch.

"Do you want a toasted cheese sandwich?" I asked.

She didn't respond.

I cooked up mine—American cheese—and ate half of it while I cooked one for her—American and cheddar, just the way she liked it. She wouldn't be able to resist. I threw it on a plate and brought it over to her. Her gaze rose to mine, and the curl in her lip softened when she saw the gooey American sandwiching the cheddar's deeper orange. It never fully melted like the American cheese did.

"Thanks," she said as she took the plate and placed it on top of her book. "Knowing how to make my favorite sandwich doesn't make you any less of a nuisance, you know."

"Yeah, yeah, I know," I told her as I sat on the chair across from her and finished my remaining half.

I stared at her full lips while she ate. A string of cheese caught on her chin, and I fought a smirk beneath my knuckle. I'd never hated Harley, even though she'd say differently. Even though I didn't like her dad, she was okay. Unlike my mother—who started acting like a spoiled brat the moment she got her hands on some of their money—Harley was shy and insecure. I was surprised she even went to that damn party.

I was the big brother, and she was the little sister. Harassing her was just a part of growing up together. I probably took it too far a time or two, and eventually she just flat out ignored me. Before the incident, she disliked me. After the incident, she hated me. By then, there was no breaking through the walls she'd built around herself with the bricks I'd handed her.

CHAPTER 8

Harley

Aside from the pest living with me, the week had been uneventful. There had been little progress in my calculus skills, and I saw it all over Ellie's face as she sat across from me at the table.

"I got this, Ellie," I told her with a halfhearted smile.

"You don't got this, Harley."

I rubbed the bridge of my nose. "I know."

"What's the matter, Hal?" The voice behind me was the last one I wanted to hear right then.

Ellie's gaze snapped up to Mason before mine did. She sat up taller and brushed her long blonde hair over her shoulder.

Don't even think about it, Ellie. I turned to look at Mason. "Nothing you need to worry about," I told him. He nodded and went scrounging around the kitchen.

"Who's that?" Ellie whispered.

"My stepbrother, Mason. He's just visiting." I returned my attention to the book to avoid more questions.

Mason came over and sat in the vacant chair between us. "What's up, ladies?" He peeled an orange and ate it. Juice dribbled down his chin when he bit into a piece, and I rolled my eyes as Ellie nearly knocked over her drink to hand him a napkin. I would never understand why women fell to his feet like that. He was a tool.

Yeah, actually, I did know why. That damn smirk of his. Mason was good-looking, but I couldn't get past the rest of him to find him attractive. Even so, I fell prey to that smirk sometimes.

"Do you like parties?" Ellie asked as she crossed her legs and leaned closer to him. I scoffed. Life was so easy for him. I practically had to beg for an invite to that party.

"I'm not really the party type," Mason said as he threw another slice of orange into his mouth. I almost laughed out loud. Mason was a textbook party-type. That's how he got into trouble in the first place. He turned to me. "Are you going?" he asked, and I stifled my laugh.

"I guess. I got myself a costume this time." I said this last part to Ellie, but she didn't even acknowledge me. She was too enamored with Mason. Gross.

"Well, if you want to go, the address is . . ." She grabbed Mason's arm and wrote on the inside of it with the pen she'd been holding.

He nodded and put the final slice into his mouth, squeezing it between his teeth. "Been fun, ladies. Be safe tonight."

"I guess," Ellie said, and she showcased her disappointment by brushing her books off the table and into her bag. Oof. If she only knew who Mason really was, she'd be glad he wasn't tagging along.

Last Mistake

Mason

I TRIED A LITTLE HARDER TO FIT IN THIS TIME. A FITTED BLACK T-shirt instead of a hoodie, jeans, and my same mask. I drove to the party and again parked down the road. When I went inside the house, I was certain I'd find Harley in an instant. She went as an 80s girl. The colors were nauseatingly loud—bright purple headband on her head, neon green crop top that hung off her shoulder. Despite this, I struggled to find her. I moved through the house, searching for her. Panic quickened my heartbeat. Was I too late?

I finally spotted her, leaning against the wall and looking really fucking sad. When she saw me, she smiled and waved in a way she never did toward Mason. There was no sign of Jeff, so I thought about backing away and leaving. No need to make this any messier than it already was.

"Guy!" she called as I backed away. The confused strangle at hearing my fake name made me stop dead in my tracks. She hurried over and gave me a hug. I recognized her warmth the instant she touched me. "I was hoping you'd show up! And I'm sober this time... mostly."

I lowered my voice again. "Good," I said.

"What?" she shouted, leaning toward me. "I can't hear you over this music." She looked around. "Let's go back to the bedroom! Quieter there."

Everything in me told me no. She was safe. Time to leave. But I let her tug me down the hall anyway. When we got into the bedroom, she closed the door and locked it. I didn't know what she thought would happen, but it wouldn't be *that*. When she sat by the bedside lamp, I saw the glaze covering her eyes. She wasn't drunk, but she was *something*. I walked over to her and lifted her chin, forcing her makeup-encased eyes to meet mine.

"What are you on?" I asked. She pouted her lip at me, and I was struck by how fucking beautiful and innocent she looked at that moment. But I knew it was only because she wasn't looking at me. The real me. "What'd you take, Ha—" I stopped myself before I called her Hal.

"I just took an edible," she said, tugging away from my grasp.

I hated that she had absolutely no party survival skills. You didn't just accept random drinks and drugs. I knew what happened when girls did. "Stop taking things from people at parties," I said, sounding much harsher than I meant to. "You know better."

She cocked her head at me, and I blew out a breath as I sat beside her. The edible, or whatever the hell it was, was hitting her harder. She dropped her head against me, and I caught it before she fell into my lap.

Come on, Hal.

I wasn't the babysitting type. Never had been, even when we were kids. I glanced at her bare knee, at a scar caused by my inattentiveness. I brushed a hand through her messy hair. I was a bad brother most of the time. I knew that. But I was trying to be better.

The moment I tried to help her into bed, she seemed to get her second wind. "Kiss me," she demanded. That was a big fucking nope.

"You're high. I'm not kissing you," I said as I drew away from her. She was my damn sister.

"Please?" she begged.

Everything in me said it was a bad idea—screamed it, actually—but I struggled to ignore it. There was something in me that wanted her affection, even if it wasn't for *me*. I wouldn't sleep with her or go further than a kiss, but in that moment, while she was high and I was incredibly stupid, I gave in.

I turned off the light and removed my mask in the darkness. I leaned into her and pulled her by the back of the neck toward my mouth. She smelled like familiarity. Like family. But she didn't feel familiar.

Cupping her face in my hands, I kissed her in a way that was so much more tender than I ever thought I could be. She whimpered against my mouth, and it made me hard. I ached against my zipper.

When she reached toward my lap, I didn't see it. I only felt it once she grabbed me. I broke our kiss and pushed her hand away. That was a line I wouldn't cross. Couldn't.

CHAPTER 9

Mason

I didn't cross that line. How could I? I would've taken advantage of her in more ways than one. She was high, and she wanted to sleep with this mysterious stranger, not me. Not Mason. If I'd gone through with it and she'd found out, I'd be exactly what she always said I was.

She sat beside me in my car, and her gaze remained locked on the floor in front of her. I was surprised she was upset. She'd rammed my past down my throat for years, but now she was asking me to do something no better—and in some ways worse—than what happened at that party.

"What's the matter?" I asked.

"Do you find me unattractive?" she asked without lifting her gaze.

Well, shit. How would I answer that?

Harley was a beautiful girl, but the hellish history between us made it hard for me to think about. "You've been fucked-up both times I've seen you, Harley." I put the car in drive and left the curb to head toward her house.

"What if I'm sober next time?" she asked, and her eyes finally rose to mine. Or at least, to the eyes on my mask.

"I'll consider it, sweet girl."

I placed my hand in hers, and she looked at the inside of my arm. Before she could ask about the inky splotches, I released her hand and gripped the steering wheel. I'd forgotten about the address. It was mostly smeared off, but I couldn't risk her figuring out my identity. I liked how she talked to me when I was Guy. I felt very little for other people, but I was starting to really care for her in ways I shouldn't. The problem was that she hated me, and in a couple more weeks, there'd be no way to wear a mask to hide who I was. This would have to end.

"Can I text you?" she asked as we pulled into her driveway.

I cursed under my breath. I worried she'd ask for my number. I had a phone app that gave me a new number, but I didn't use it for casual conversations. Mostly it was to sell a little pot here and there when I had the stuff.

Her eyes rounded with sadness when I didn't respond, and the weight of the rejection she felt pressed down on my chest. *God damn it.* I caved and gave her that number, which she put into her phone.

"See you next week? Maybe?" she asked.

"Maybe."

I pulled out of the driveway, took off my mask, and drove to a nearby parking lot. I stayed there for a while, a cigarette dangling from my lips as I listened to music. The more I thought about what I'd gotten myself into, the worse I felt. My phone chimed. I picked it up and saw a number that wasn't in the app but was in my mind. Harley.

> Hey. Thanks for being a gentleman again. Sorry I was a mess.

I wondered if I should reply. I kept ignoring all my reason around her; what's one more time?

> It's okay. I'm serious though. Stop taking things at parties. There are men who go to those parties looking for messy girls like you ;)

> Oh, I know, I'm related to one of them.

Ouch.

I dropped my phone like it was on fire. No matter what I did or didn't do to Harley, she'd never forgive me. Even though we could get along fine if I wasn't me, Mason was still nothing to her. Worse than nothing. I threw a sweater jacket over my shirt, zipped it up, and walked back toward her house. I knocked before going inside.

"Hey," I said as I closed the door.

She was sitting on the couch with her phone in her hands. She dropped it onto her lap and my phone chimed. I reached into my pocket and put my phone on vibrate, then went straight to my room. I stared at my phone once I'd stripped out of my sweater and T-shirt.

> Tell me something about you?

Half of me wanted to ignore the message. The other half wanted to give her a chance to get to know me.

> I'm a sucker for poetry.

> Not much for poems but love reading. Maybe you can show me some poems you like?

> I actually write them.

> Swoon. You'll definitely have to read me something next time.

If Harley had spent five minutes with me, she'd have realized I wasn't the big, stupid inconvenience she thought I was. Though to be honest, I didn't make it easy on either of us. I didn't know if I could let her in even if I wanted to at this point. She'd made me believe all the things she said over the years.

I sat on the bed and stared at my texts from her. My phone vibrated, but it wasn't a message from Harley. It was an unknown number.

> Saw your sister. She looked delicious. Can't wait to take a bite. Mystery man can't keep her safe forever.

Another text came in, and it was a picture of Harley in her bright outfit from the party, which meant he'd been there. Maybe he'd worn a different mask. Fuck. I couldn't stomach the idea of him getting his hands on her. She was the innocence he loved to take. The same innocence she was offering to me.

CHAPTER 10

Harley

Guy and I had so much in common. We both liked the same kind of music, and he had the same sense of humor as me. As I scrolled through our long string of texts, the flush on my chest told me just how much I was starting to like him. He even guessed my favorite kind of tree.

"What are you smiling about?" Mason asked from the table behind me. His phone rested on the wooden surface, tucked right against his forearm.

"Nunya," I told him, which meant it was none of his business. Which it wasn't. I blocked his view and went back to my phone.

> Please tell me you're going to the party tomorrow. I want more than a kiss. But can I tell you something?

> Of course.

> I've never done anything else...

My concentration broke when glass shattered behind me. I sat up and saw Mason picking up the shards of a coffee mug.

"What the hell, Mason?" I snapped.

"The mug's handle broke," he said as he stood to clean up the mess. "Fuck." A thin stream of blood dripped from his hand.

I threw down my phone and went to help him. I grabbed his hand and studied the gash in his palm. He cursed under his breath as I wrapped his hand with paper towels.

"You okay?" I asked him. He was acting weird. "You're so jumpy."

"I'm fine."

"You're not, but okay." I released his hand, and he drew it toward his chest.

He shook his head. "Sorry, Hal." I bent down to pick up his phone, but he intercepted it.

I narrowed my eyes on him. He was being really fucking weird. Weirder than usual. I had no choice but to let it go. Soon, he'd be out of my hair and not breaking my favorite fucking mugs.

Mason

I mopped up the coffee with a hand towel and swept the glass into a dustpan before discarding it in the trash. The dark-roast aroma wafted up to me as I wrung out the towel in the sink. It was twice as hard with only one hand, and I left tan splatters from the table to the garbage.

"I'll clean up the rest," Harley said with a groan. "Go take care of your hand."

I went to the bathroom and washed my hands with soap and water. Red and pink streaks tinged the porcelain. I put a Band-Aid over the gash before going to the bedroom to change my shirt. I shrugged off the coffee-stained T-shirt and put on a fresh one.

Still in a daze, I looked at the text on my phone again.

> I've never done anything else...

That fact did several conflicting things to me. First, it terrified me. Jeff would prey on that. He'd be able to smell the innocence all over her if he got his hands on her. Second, it made me hard, and I had no idea why.

No matter how many times I read it, I couldn't keep my jaw from dropping. I always said Harley was frigid, but I didn't think she was *that* cold. Who survived through high school with their virginity intact these days? How would someone even respond to that?

And why did I want to warm her up?

I'd dropped the mug I was holding when her text came through because I *really* didn't expect that. I had no idea she'd never done anything with anyone, but why would I have asked? The worst part? I left her on read. She probably thought Guy wanted nothing to do with her after she'd admitted that.

I picked up my phone and fought the twisting of my stomach so I could respond.

> Sorry for my late response. I didn't know what to say to that, and I don't want to say anything wrong. Why are you telling me that?

> Well... Never mind.

> Tell me.

> Just wondered if you wanted to be my first...

Jesus Christ, Harley. I wanted to go in there, rip the phone out of her hand, and ask her what the fuck she thought she was doing. Why would she hand that over to Guy . . . to me?

> Why? You haven't even seen my face. You don't even know me.

> True. Will you show me your face?

> I can't. I'm insecure about how I look.

She started and stopped typing several times. Then I stayed on read. I put down my phone and blew out a breath as I rubbed at my injured palm. My phone vibrated, and I picked it up with my injured hand without thinking.

> We can keep the lights off? ;)

A smile crossed my face, and my belly tingled with more than just the usual nausea from the mess I'd created. Harley was something else when she wasn't putting all her energy into hating Mason. My fingers flew over the screen.

> I'll consider it, sweet girl.

Would I? Part of me wanted to—the part that wanted to devour her innocence so that no one else could—but the rest of me said I shouldn't. If I went through with it, I just had to make sure she never knew it was me. She could never find out because it would destroy us both. Guy could take her the way she asked. The way she deserved. I would make her feel better than any young college kid could.

As long as I was just the faceless stranger from the college party, I could fuck Harley.

I reached down and rubbed my uninjured hand along the length of my shaft. It caught on the barbell pierced through my frenum. I looked around before tugging down my sweatpants and boxers, then snapped a quick picture and sent it to her.

> Be sure this is what you want before you touch me next time ;)

"What!" Harley screamed from the other room.

I pulled up my pants and walked into the living room to check on her. "Are you okay? Why are you yelling?" I asked.

Her jaw was still dropped, lips parted in shock. A bright flush colored her cheeks, and I kind of liked that it was because of my dick.

She shook her head. "I . . . just got some grades back," she stammered. It was fucking adorable.

I'd leave it up to her. If she touched me, she'd do so knowing what I could do to her.

CHAPTER 11

Harley

As I leaned against the wall at the party, the music thrumming through my body, I waited for him to appear. I waved off anyone who tried to hand me anything because I'd promised I'd remain sober for him.

I scrolled through our texts as I waited, stopping at his dick picture. I stared at the black barbell, and it equally excited and scared me. He was big, which was already intimidating enough, but he was also pierced. I had no idea what that metal would feel like.

Like a ghost, he appeared out of nowhere. The moment I saw him, my stomach tightened. I had promised him my body, but now that seemed terrifying. When I took a step toward him, he just gestured toward the bedrooms.

I walked down the hall, and I felt him behind me. His presence made my hair stand up. He felt dangerous. I began to regret ever making this suggestion as he came in behind me and closed the door. Unlike every other time he brought me into a room, his hands were on me the instant the door snicked shut. The fingers of one hand sank into the flesh of my breast through the thin cami, and the other dropped down my pants. It was too fast. It was all moving too fast. I gripped his shirt and tried to push him away, but he only growled and threw me onto the bed.

"Stop, Guy!" I yelled as I writhed beneath his weight.

His palm clamped over my mouth as he unzipped his pants. His hand roved up my skirt. I'd worn the silky black fabric just for him. The cat ears that were perched on my head dislodged and fell beside me. The little whiskers I'd drawn with eyeliner were surely smeared across my cheeks now.

Tears welled and slipped past his hand. I cursed myself for trusting this strange man with my body. With my virginity. It wasn't supposed to happen like this.

His weight was ripped off me, and he was thrown to the ground. A man with the same mask towered over the one on the floor. He sent a kick into his side that made him curl up on himself. I covered my mouth to keep from screaming as my savior leaped on my tormentor and started to choke him.

He ripped off the man's mask and punched him in the face. Blood soaked his features, obscuring them entirely.

"Are you okay?" the man on top asked me.

The voice sounded familiar, so low and comforting, but I couldn't respond. I couldn't trust myself anymore.

Guy leaned over the man. "If you ever touch her again, so help me god, I'll kill you." He shook the man beneath him. "Do you understand me?"

Mason

"It's not over," Jeff snarled, low enough that only I could hear, but I didn't have time to fuck with him. I had to take care of Harley. I needed to see if she was okay.

"Get the fuck out," I hissed and climbed off him.

He scrambled out of the room, and I locked the door behind him. I rubbed my blood-covered knuckles before walking toward her. With her knees drawn toward her chest as she cowered on the bed, she looked so small and vulnerable.

Fucking Jeff. What a genius idea for such a stupid man.

"Harley," I whispered as I approached her. She kept shaking her head. I reached out to touch her face, and she recoiled. "Did he hurt you?"

"No," she whispered. "How do I even know it's you?" Her eyes were full of mistrust. Her chest continued to rise and fall with each panicked breath.

How the hell could I prove it to her? She'd never seen my face, and I couldn't remove the mask, even if I'd wanted to. There was only one way I could prove who I was, and it wasn't ideal after what she'd just been through. I sighed and unzipped my jeans, and her eyes widened as I stroked myself beneath the denim.

"What are you—" she started, but I cut her off as I pulled out my dick. I grabbed her hand, and despite the tension in her arm as she tried to pull away, I ran her fingers up the underside of my cock. The corners of her lips lifted as her fingers grazed the barbell.

"The worst way to show you, I know. But it's me."

She rose onto her knees and kept her hand on me. "You saved me," she whispered.

I hadn't saved her. I was the reason all of this was happening to her in the first place. It was all my fault.

When I'd gotten to the party and hadn't seen her, I'd panicked. I searched for her everywhere before I went down the hall and heard her voice. Her whimpers. Then I saw the man wearing my mask as he pressed himself on top of her, and I knew exactly who it was. I couldn't let her see his face, and it took everything inside me not to kill him right then.

Her hand burned the skin of my dick. I wanted to pull it away from her and stop the guilt already ripping through me. Instead, I brushed my fingertips along her cheek, where her makeup had smeared. Her icy-blue eyes rolled up, and she bit her lip.

"What do you want, sweet girl?" I asked.

"Will this hurt me?"

I didn't know. I'd never been inside someone as innocent as her.

I sighed. "I'm not sure."

She seemed so breakable. So fragile. I fought the urge to kiss her because I had no way of doing so with my mask on. Trying to tell myself this was transactional, that it would be better for her to lose her innocence to someone who wouldn't destroy her, wasn't working.

"I know what it won't hurt," I said as I sat down beside her. "Give me your mouth." I'd asked Harley to give me so many things over the years, but nothing like what I was asking her for now. It was sick. So fucking wrong. But I couldn't stop.

A glint of confusion and nerves washed over her, and she dropped her gaze. I guided her off the bed and helped her to her knees. Seeing her like that—wide-eyed with curiosity as my dick rose in front of her face—made me twitch.

I balled her hair at the back of her neck and brought her mouth toward me. "Open up, Harley," I whispered as her lips touched the hot skin of my dick.

She swallowed hard and spread her lips to take me into her mouth. Her tongue pressed against my piercing and made me shiver.

"God," I groaned, letting her explore me at her own pace. She felt incredible. I wished it felt worse.

I gripped her hair and guided her along my length. Usually I would have preferred to grab the back of her head and fuck her throat, but Harley was sweet innocence, and I let her tongue work me as she toyed with my piercing.

Harley pulled her mouth away, and drool clung to her lower lip. I'd never seen someone so damn beautiful, and it was a sucker punch to my morals. Any ethical bone in my body disintegrated at the sight of her. I released her hair and ran my hand along her face. She reached up and pulled it away to examine it.

"What happened to your hand?"

Panic roared inside me. I still had a Band-Aid over the cut in my palm. I hoped she wouldn't put two and two together. Not after her mouth had already been on my dick.

"It's nothing, just a cut," I told her.

She nodded, and I pulled her off her knees to keep her from asking any more questions. I trailed my hands up her bare thighs, beneath the little skirt I wanted her to wear like a good girl. Her skin pebbled beneath my touch. I gripped her ass, and she released the softest moan. One hand left her ass, and I tugged her panties aside. I growled as I finally touched what was between her legs. The warm wetness coating her. It was all for me.

She gasped as I rubbed along her slit. I pulled her onto my lap, and her thighs encased mine. The skirt rode up, and the heat of her pussy hovered so close to my dick that it made me throb.

"Guy," she whispered through a moan as my fingers worked her swollen clit. I wished she was saying my name. I wanted to hear the pleasure woven through it like that. She dripped on my dick, and I twitched beneath her.

"I want to feel you," I growled.

She tensed, and I thought she might change her mind. It was too late to change mine. Her hands reached for my mask, but I gripped the bottom of it, keeping her from tugging it off and seeing who I was.

"Leave it on." I pulled her hands away from my face. "You sure you want this?" I gripped my dick and moved my hand up the shaft in a long stroke.

She nodded, and I rubbed the head of my dick through her slit and moved toward her entrance. I gripped her hips and lowered her onto me, as slow and easy as I could. I was overwhelmed by her. The whimper of pain that left her lips, the way her pussy fought my dick before letting me inside, and her fingers digging into my shoulders as she took me like a good girl.

Pangs of guilt followed. I'd intended to use a condom with her. I'd planned on it until the heat of her pussy pressed against my bare skin. Then I'd wanted nothing more than to push inside her. I wouldn't come inside her—that I could promise her—but I needed to feel her. All of her.

"Are you okay?" I asked.

"It hurts," she whimpered, her body tensing on my lap. I'd worried it would.

I brushed a hand through her hair. "Push through the pain, sweet girl. Next time it'll feel better."

She met my gaze. I shouldn't have said that. I couldn't

guarantee there would be a next time when there shouldn't have been a *first* time. I was being selfish enough by taking her body once, and to do it again would be much too risky. Too stupid. It would be almost impossible to stop myself from doing it again, but I'd have to try.

I lay back and lifted my hips to push myself deeper into her. To force her to work through that pain so she could stretch around me and start to feel good. I put my hand between us and rubbed her clit, and eventually she forgot the pain and focused on the pleasure. Soon her hips moved with mine, and I couldn't wait to feel how she would truly move with me once she got used to my dick.

There I go again, planning the next time I can lay her on her back, when I should be trying to figure out how to end our forbidden tryst.

A moan escaped Harley's lips, and my balls tightened. I grabbed her hips and stopped either of us from moving. I didn't want to come inside her, and that was exactly what would've happened if she kept looking and feeling like that.

We were motionless except for my fingers once I put them back on her clit. I rubbed her until she fought my grip on her hip and her pussy clenched around me. She came, and I had to push her off my lap to keep from coming inside her. I wrapped a hand around the base of my dick and climbed over her. She inhaled a shallow breath, and I leaned over to flip the light off before I ripped off my mask.

I needed her mouth on mine.

I found her lips in the dark and kissed her. She whimpered as her hands rode up my chest. I stroked myself against her bare pussy and came on her soft skin. "Harley," I growled against her mouth. I reached down and pulled her panties over her, concealing her come-covered pussy. My fingers grazed her wet slit through her panties, and she jolted.

I rolled onto my back and pulled her against my chest. She blew out a pleasure-soaked breath. There was so much more I wanted to do to her, but I could hardly handle being inside her like that. Her body was electric, and I was the fuse trying to keep that electricity at a safe level. None of this was safe, though.

"Wear my come, sweet girl," I said as I kissed the top of her head.

"Is this the end?" she asked.

The question rattled me. I was torn between saying yes and no. Torn between being moral and immoral. I wanted to say yes, that I just wanted to take what she offered before anyone else could take it from her, but I felt compelled to say no because I needed more time with her.

"I don't think so," I said. I compromised because I wanted to end it but couldn't. I left it open so I could consider the gravity of what I'd done and fully appreciate the weight of fucking my stepsister, a person who disliked everything about me. Well, almost everything.

"You knew who that man was, didn't you?" she asked after I stroked her hair for so long that I forgot where we were.

Of course I did, but I couldn't tell her that. "No, I don't know who he is."

"He said it's not over. What isn't over?"

"I don't know, sweet girl, but I'll protect you from whatever *it* is." I ran a firm hand down her arm to soothe the start of trembles.

I would protect her. I just needed to figure out how.

CHAPTER 12

Harley

I sat at the kitchen table with half of my mind focused on the textbook in front of me. The other half wouldn't stop reliving what had happened last night. I raised my phone and sent a text.

> Thank you for last night

> Don't thank me. It's weird ;)

Mason came into the kitchen, half naked except for the gray sweatpants hugging his hips. I closed my textbook and eyed him. "ETA on your apartment?"

"Good morning to you too," he said as he rifled through the cabinets.

"I'm serious, Mason. I'd like to have my house back."

"Soon, I'm sure," he said as he slammed another cupboard loud enough to make me jump.

"Jesus, Mary, and Joseph! Must you be so annoying?"

He walked over to me, stepping closer until his Adonis

belt hovered right beside my head. I swallowed hard. He leaned over and rubbed a firm hand along the back of my neck. The touch felt familiar, but I couldn't understand why. We'd never been close enough to comfort each other this way.

"Annoying you is too much fun, Hal," he whispered in my ear, and his warm breath sent shivers up my body. "Why do you hate me so much?"

My eyes narrowed, and I drew away from his touch. "You know why."

"Do you hate me, or are you afraid of me?"

I scoffed. "I hate you," I said, but I wasn't sure if that was the whole of it.

I'd feared him when the police took him to the station. I remembered finding out what he'd done and telling my father I didn't want him to stay with us anymore. Rapist, abuser, dangerous. I called him every name in the book. My father just kept saying, *"He's a kid. He's a teenager."*

I was a kid. I was a teenager. And I never assaulted someone. I also didn't watch multiple men assault someone and say nothing.

Mason was a bad person, and I hated him for all he'd put me through. It was like he preyed on my fear of him before he moved out. He'd corner me or make sure he touched me when he talked to me.

"I think you're afraid of me." He leaned into me and put his hand on my shoulder. "Your breaths quicken when I'm near you. When I touch you, I see the throb of your rapid heartbeat in your neck."

"N-no," I stammered.

"Yes, Hal. Say it. Say that you're afraid of me."

"No," I said more firmly. I refused to give him that satisfaction.

Last Mistake

His hand rose from my shoulder to my throat. His voice was breathy. "Are you afraid I'll touch you?" Like a predator with its prey in its grasp, he groaned at my suffering.

A tear squeezed past my clenched eyelids, and I grabbed his wrist and pushed him away. I rose from my chair and cleared my throat to force my confidence. "Yes, Mason, I'm scared of you. Things you used to do to annoy me took on a new meaning in my head, things from before you even did what you did. You used to straddle me and tickle me to try to get me to pee my pants! You dragged me into a closet and played seven seconds in heaven after seeing it in a movie. You kissed me all over my face. Then, when you did what you did, I wondered how much of that other stuff you did with another idea in mind!"

Mason's harsh gaze softened. "I didn't even touch your lips when I played that game. You really think I'd put you on your back just to touch you like that while we were kids?" He took a quick breath and shook his head. "I didn't know you thought such horrible shit about me. You're stripping away the innocence of our childhood and making it something else, something sick, because of a mistake I made at seventeen."

My lip quivered, and I backed away from him. He paced, brushing a hand through his messy blond hair. "Do you want to know the truth about that night?" he asked.

I didn't respond.

"We were all drinking. They encouraged me to kiss her. I did. I did that to her. She started getting sleepy, and I tried to sit her down on the couch. They called me a pussy. Called me every fucking name imaginable as I tried to back away from her. To get away from what was happening, I told them I needed a drink. When I went back in the room, Jeff's friend had already started in on her. When he finished, Jeff tried to get me to take a turn. I lied and said I'd had too much to drink and couldn't get hard, and he told me to sit and watch if I couldn't participate." Mason swallowed hard. "I watched the girl's face as Jeff unzipped his pants and raped her. I wanted to stop it, and I planned to, but when I told him I had to leave, he threatened to hurt you if I didn't sit down. So I did. I fucking did." He stepped toward me and caged me between both his hands on the wall beside my head.

I flinched.

"I didn't sit there enjoying it. I wanted to stop it. But it was that girl or *you*."

"Mason . . ." I whispered. I didn't know if I believed it, but I'd never heard this part of the story.

"Don't, Hal. I *thought* I made the right choice, but the guilt ate away at me. So I told the police where they could find a recording. Convinced the girl to file an official complaint—"

My mouth gaped. "There's a recording?"

"Of the whole thing. Including me whining about my limp dick."

"You told the police? Didn't you know you'd get in trouble?"

"I guess I didn't think it through. I was naïve and thought Jeff and his buddies would get in trouble and that would be it. I didn't expect to end up in juvie because of it." He took a step back, giving me space. "But even knowing what I know now, I'd still have told them about the video."

My ears were deceiving me. I was certain of it. Did Mason actually have a heart? Was he capable of knowing right from wrong? Could he be that selfless? I'm not sure I'd have believed anything he said, even if he'd tried to tell me back then. He'd walled himself off after the incident, and his isolation had seemed like guilt to me.

"Mason," I called after him as he stormed out of the kitchen.

He came back out dressed in his work clothes, and I got in front of him.

"Move, Harley."

"Will you wait? We need to talk about this." I didn't know he'd tried to protect me. I had no idea. How could I have?

"There's nothing to talk about." His eyes narrowed. "I'd move you myself, but I don't want you to worry about me raping you since you seem to think that's my entire motive for ever touching you." He spat the words, and I recoiled.

He'd wanted me to admit I feared him. He'd forced the truth out of me, and now he was mad about it.

"Fuck you, Mason! Don't ask me questions if you aren't prepared to hear the answers!" I screamed at him as he pushed past me. He slammed the door in my face and left me bathing in a confusing wash of guilt and anguish.

CHAPTER 13

Mason

Harley sent me another text, but I wasn't in the mood to respond. She made me feel like I was a disgusting man. Like I could ever take advantage of her like that.

You are taking advantage of her, yelled my conscience. I groaned and rubbed between my eyes. It was true. I was. I just wish she hadn't felt so good, so right, because she was so wrong.

I looked at the text again.

> Are you mad at me?

I sighed and stuffed my phone into my pocket.

Work went by uneventfully, which was good. It needed to. The break was good for me. I drove home but took a left instead of a right. I had to confront something—well, some*one*—before I went back to Harley's.

I drove to the outskirts of the city and pulled into the crumbling driveway in front of the familiar run-down mobile home. Jeff had grown up in the same neighborhood I had. I got out of the car and took a deep breath as I knocked on the door. He opened it and stared at me. Bruises covered the skin around his eyes and the bridge of his nose.

"What happened to your face?" I asked, even though I knew what happened to his stupid face. *I* happened to him.

"Your sister's little mystery man does a better job at protecting her than you do," he taunted.

"Leave Harley alone, Jeff. I heard what happened at the party. You're lucky it wasn't me, because if I had seen it, I would have killed you."

"Kill me then, Mason. Take your shot. Or are you still too much of a pussy?" He leaned closer, and the liquor on his breath invaded my personal space.

"I've already gone to jail because of you once, but if you assault my sister again, any jury will understand why I killed you. No sane person would feel bad that someone like *you* had been taken out." I pushed him back, and he fell into his doorway. "Stay the fuck away from her."

I went back to my car, unconvinced that he'd leave her alone. If anything, he'd want to get to her more. But I'd needed to confront him. I needed him to know what I'd do to protect Harley, even after everything she'd said.

My phone buzzed.

> I'm sorry for whatever I did.

> I'm sorry I keep texting. I'm just having a really emotional night.

> You didn't do anything. What's wrong?

> Family shit. Can I see you?

Last Mistake

> That's not a good idea.

My phone stayed silent after that.

I drove to Harley's house, lost in my head. I'd admitted all that went down that night. I'd spilled my guts to her. She should fucking feel bad for thinking anything I did to her when we were younger was sexual. I never saw her that way. I didn't see her that way until that night at the first party. Yeah, sure, I'd catch a glimpse of her cleavage every so often and I'd pop a boner, but those tits could have been attached to anyone and I'd have probably still gotten hard. But I'd never specifically thought of Harley's chest until I had the chance to touch it.

I parked in the lot down the road and walked inside. Harley sat up on the couch, and despite her best attempts to hide it, I could see she'd been crying. She wiped at her red, splotchy cheeks.

I walked over to her, kneeled down, and instinctively grabbed her hand. "It wasn't a big deal, Harley. I wouldn't have said anything if I knew it would upset you this much."

She ripped her hand away from me. "I'm not upset about you," she snapped.

I stood up. "About what, then?"

"Nothing," she said as she sat back and dropped her gaze.

"Talk to me," I whispered, trying to get her to open up to me, even though I knew she wouldn't. I knew who she would open up to, though. When she wouldn't meet my gaze, I knew she needed Guy.

I patted her shoulder, went to the kitchen table, and took a seat. I put my phone on silent and set it down in front of me.

> Hey

I waited for her response. I knew she'd seen the text. I heard the buzz and saw her check her phone. But the message status remained unread. Just as I was about to get up and go to my room, I saw the quiet notification pop up on my screen.

> Why do you think we aren't a good idea?

Because she hated me? Because she was my stepsister?

> Because you can't ever see my face. And you deserve more than a man in a mask.

> I'd stay in the dark for you.

My cheeks flushed at her words. Harley had stopped crying. That was a good thing, at least.

She had no clue who she was trying to be with. She'd never accept the man beneath the mask. So why did I feel like giving in to her? Why did I feel the need to give her everything she wanted and more? Especially after how she thought of me. How little she thought of who I was.

Who I am.

Why did I think she deserved more when she thought I deserved so little?

> What if I told you to meet me under the footbridge by the river on Halloween night? What would you say?

I couldn't bring her to the last party of the Halloween season. Jeff would be lurking.

> What are you going to do to me?

> Depends. I'll let you choose whether you truly want to stay in the dark with me or not.

> If you're going to be wearing a mask, should I dress up too?

> Wear that skirt, no panties this time. Aside from that? Wear whatever the hell else you want, sweet girl.

Harley did not deserve the best of Guy when she thought so poorly of me. I'd be rougher with her. Take her into the dark and show her it wasn't where she wanted to be. She could break it off with Guy, and we could be done with it. We had to be done with it. What was happening couldn't keep happening, no matter how much either of us liked it. One of these days, she'd realize Guy and I were one and the same.

And our lives would be ruined.

CHAPTER 14

Harley

The cold fall air bit at my skin as I waited beneath the entrance to the footbridge. Beautiful stone architecture lifted the bridge for the people to walk above me. I shifted my weight, trying to calm my nerves and warm the chill coating my skin. I clutched my jacket closer to my body. Squeals of laughter came from the distance, reminding me that it was Halloween.

Footsteps behind me sent a strangling jolt of anticipation through my body. My breath hitched as I turned and saw him.

Guy.

His mask was lifted just enough to allow him to smoke a cigarette beneath it. When he saw me, he threw the cigarette to the ground and squelched it beneath his boot.

"Hey, sweet girl," he said. His words warmed me in an instant and heated me to my very core. He circled me. "So dangerous out here for someone like you," he teased, rubbing one of the cat ears on my headband.

"I knew you were coming," I said.

He used his body to usher me against the stone wall. "What makes you think I'm safe, Harley? You said you wanted to go into the dark with me," he growled. His hands landed on either side of my head, and my breath caught in my throat. "You seem scared. Are you scared of me?" he asked. I was too enamored with the low gravel in his voice to even acknowledge what he'd asked.

He grabbed my shoulder, turned me around, and pushed me against the wall with his body. His hands glided down my sides until they reached my hips, and he used them to pop my ass out for him. Rocks crunched as he went down on his knees, and before I even knew what was happening, his plastic mask grazed my bare pussy. I didn't realize he'd raised it and let it rest on his forehead until I felt his mouth on me. I gasped. The plastic crinkled along my skin as he moved his tongue against me. My nails dug into the rough rock as he worked me in ways I never thought possible.

The sensations were all new, but even without knowing what it was supposed to feel like, I knew he was doing a good job. His tongue was an expert. A moan left my lips and broke the silence.

His mask crinkled as he drew his tongue away to speak. "Shh, sweet girl."

The moment the last syllable left his lips, he was back on my clit. I lurched when he put two of his fingers inside me. I tried to move my hips with him, but his steadfast grip held me in place.

"Come on my mask," he growled through another long lash of his tongue across my slit. He licked me and thrust his fingers in and out of me until I had to bite my own hand to keep from screaming out. He made me come hard against his face, his mask sliding along my wetness.

He turned me around, and I looked up at the neon *X*'s that hid his eyes because he'd lowered his mask again. My come glistened on the plastic. "Clean my mask," he said as his wet fingers rode up the back of my neck and fisted my hair. "Lick it off."

He drew me toward his mouth, and I licked at my own come, cleaning off the mask that had ground along my slit. A low growl left his throat, and I thought for a moment that he might remove the mask and kiss me.

Instead, he said, "That wasn't darkness, Harley. That was just the tunnel before. True darkness doesn't come until I'm inside you."

Mason

She smelled like coconut and her come. I wished I could take off my mask to kiss her. To devour her. But I couldn't.

Her eyes widened as I leaned my body into hers and unzipped my jeans. I pulled out my cock and put her cold hand on me. Her grip swirled around my head, and her fingers ran along my piercing. I wanted her mouth on me, but I needed her pussy more. I couldn't last long with her last time. Her tight, untouched pussy was too fucking much. I wanted more of that. Her mouth, if she ever spoke to Guy again, would be there for me to use another night.

"Guy," she whispered as nerves choked off the end of my pseudonym.

I didn't give her a chance to protest further, just pushed her against the rocks, pulled up her skirt, and lifted her thigh. I pushed inside her, her warmth more noticeable against the cold night air. She whimpered as I went deep. Her pussy was more inviting this time around. I covered her mouth with one hand, let the other fall to steady her hip, and fucked her like she deserved. I thrust up and into her as if I hated her the way she hated me.

I fought the urge to tell her that the things she'd said had hurt me. They'd brought me to the point of wanting to not only make her feel good, but to return some of the pain she'd caused me.

Her eyes glossed and her body tightened as my dick hurt her in ways she wasn't used to, but even through the pain, she tilted her pelvis against me. A tear fell from the corner of her right eye, and it took everything in me not to wipe it from her cheek. But I needed her to hate me and move on with her happy little life without me . . . or Guy.

She tensed around me and I stalled, my hips flush against her warmth as I tried to keep from coming. I pulled my hand away from her mouth and rubbed my finger along her lower lip.

"You like the dark, don't you?" I asked her. She nodded and her body relaxed again. I repeatedly drew back my hips, leaving just the tip inside her, and her opening grazed against my piercing with every pass. "If we're going to keep doing this, I'll need you to do something for me," I whispered.

She nodded much too fast.

"Get on birth control. I don't care what kind. I just need to be able to come inside this perfect fucking pussy of yours." I didn't leave room for her to protest as I drew my hips back and punctuated my point with a hard thrust.

"I will," she whispered through a panting breath.

"Promise?"

"I promise."

I couldn't hold back any longer. I drew my hips back a final time, my come spilling from me the moment I left her warm pussy, and I rubbed it along her slit. She dropped back her head as I spread her lips with the head of my dick and rubbed her clit.

I eased away from her, tucked myself into my pants, and lowered her skirt. "Such a good girl," I told her. I fought the urge to take off my mask and kiss her; the moonlight made everything too light, even beneath the footbridge, and I couldn't let her see my face. "Let's get you home." I grabbed her hand and we walked toward my car. I opened the door for her, and she shifted her weight instead of getting inside.

"What's the matter?" I asked.

Her cheeks flushed. "Your come," she whispered, pointing toward her short skirt.

"So what? Sit your ass down."

I loved the idea of her come-covered pussy making a mess in my car. I loved that she had to sit there with my come dripping between her legs. My come. Not Guy's. The man she was so afraid would touch her? Yeah, that was *his* come. And next time, I'd make sure it was inside. The monster in her head became the one inside her after all.

I dropped her off and parked my car down the road. I sat there, reminiscing about her. How right and wrong she felt. The way she squeezed my dick when I first put it inside her, like her body didn't know what to do with such an intrusion. And then how she relaxed and I felt everything from within her.

My phone vibrated and took me out of the moment. It

was Harley, and she'd sent me a picture of her come-covered pussy, her inner thighs all gleaming wet. *Fuck.*

> What a mess ;)

> Fuck, sweet girl. I could get used to that.

I rubbed myself through my jeans, already hard again the moment I saw that picture. Any hope of stopping what I was doing with her flew out the fucking window. With her covered in my come, I realized what she was. She was fucking mine. Stepsiblings or not, I would devour her until I had my fill.

CHAPTER 15

Harley

It'd been a little over a week since I saw Guy and just under a week since my doctor squeezed me in for an IUD. It hurt like hell, and the only thing that kept me from breaking down at the appointment was thinking of my promise to Guy. I wanted to be his good girl. I wanted to please him.

Mason came in without even a hello thrown my way. Usually he said hi or at least barked something offensive. Loud footsteps sounded nearby, and then a door slammed.

I pushed my book off my lap and looked at my phone. I hadn't heard from Guy all day. He got weird immediately after we had sex, but then he seemed all-in once he saw me coated in his come. Now he was running cooler again. I shot him a text, unable to wait much longer to find out if I needed to get ready after all.

> Are you still coming by tonight?

> Did you take time to think about what you want to do?

> Yes, and I have a surprise for you.

> If it's not you I don't want it ;)

I laughed. He was the sweetest person, and I was falling for our late-night texts. I could get used to the dirty pictures he sent back to me. His hand wrapped around his dick. His piercing resting above his fingers. It was delicious.

I looked around before slipping a hand down my sweatpants and carrying on the conversation with Guy.

> I wish I could be between your legs right now, sweet girl.

Mason

I had a rough day at work. One of those days when nothing went right and all your energy was spent just trying to stay alive until the end of your shift.

> What would you do to me?

She sure knew how to draw me out of the solemnness of a bad day. I stared at the blinking cursor. There were so many things I'd do to Harley. I would devour her.

> I'd lay you down and fuck you with my mouth. I wouldn't stop until you came all over my face.

I tugged down the front of my pants and gripped my dick, stroking myself as we continued to talk dirty to each other. I planned to cancel tonight because of how bad today went, but how could I when she was telling me what she'd do to me? Thinking about her made my balls tighten, and I wanted to come. And I wanted to last when I fucked her later. The spilled come would buy me time.

I heard a noise that drew my attention—a sound that was familiar to me when it shouldn't have been.

I got out of bed and walked out of the room. The softest whisper floated down the hall. *She isn't!* I thought as I realized what she was doing. The slick sound and her moans. She was doing exactly what I had been doing.

I kept myself pinned to the wall as I watched her on the couch. My face flushed with renewed heat as she rubbed herself beneath her pants. My cock swelled as if it had never gone down in the first place.

Her back arched as she worked her pussy. It took everything in me to stay where I was instead of rushing to help her. To make her come. But she'd never let Mason touch her. If I was Guy, I could do anything to her.

I watched her in secret as she looked at her phone and played with herself. I tugged down my sweatpants and took my cock in my hand. Her moans fueled each stroke. As quietly as I could, I double-clicked the side of my phone to pull up my camera and snapped a pic of my cock. I sent it to her, and her phone chimed. The moan that flew from her lips at the sight of me brought me to my edge with a smirk on my face. I leaned back against the wall and listened to her come as I released into my hand.

I hadn't thought this through. I'd have to walk past her to get to the bathroom. I started back toward the room, and I heard her voice.

"Mason? Is that you?" she asked.

Fuck. Fuck. Fuck. I panicked. Her footsteps drew closer, and I clutched my hand into a fist. The sticky warmth squelched in my hand. *Am I being punished?*

I cleared my throat as she came around the corner. "Yeah, it's me. I was just going to go shower but forgot my shirt. Was just going to get it."

A relieved sigh eased out of her, and I almost smirked. She thought I'd caught her. Well, I did. But she caught me too.

She eyed me with a hint of suspicion, and I walked past her toward the bathroom. "I thought you needed a shirt?"

"Fuck it, I'll get it after," I said as I walked into the bathroom. I went to close the door, but her voice fluttered toward me.

"Is your apartment almost done?" she asked.

I took a deep breath. "Almost. Ran into some complications with some stuff being out of stock." God, I was a bad liar.

"Kinda want my house back."

"I know, Hal, and I'm working on it. I won't be here a day longer than I have to." I shut the door, turned on the shower, and rinsed my hand under the jet of water. Bald-faced lies, but worth it.

CHAPTER 16

Harley

Sweat coated my palms, so I wiped them down the black skirt I knew he liked. Guy was letting me into his home, his world. My gaze darted, trying to find his apartment. 402. I spotted the door down the hall, and hanging on the knob were two blindfolds. One was made from a thick black fabric, and the other was a mask that would ensure I couldn't see him through the gaps in the first.

My heartbeat quickened as I did what he'd told me to do over text. I wound the fabric around my head, tying it off in a knot behind me. I slipped the mask over it, and any light that had snuck through disappeared. Once I was fully masked, I knocked on the heavy metal door.

My cheeks flushed as I stood outside his door, blindfolded in a public hallway. I probably looked batty. But I was doing all this to sleep with a man whose face I'd never even seen, so maybe I was as crazy as I looked.

The door eased open, and hands tugged me inside. Guy pushed me against the wall, and a small gasp escaped my lips at the sheer excitement that came from his touch. I'd been dreaming of his hands on me. I'd touched myself to the thought of him.

"Sweet girl," he groaned as he leaned into my neck and kissed me. "I like not having the mask on. I can taste you. All of you."

"I'm not worried about how you look."

"You wouldn't like me if you knew who I was, Harley."

I pouted. "I already like you."

His kiss silenced me, his warm lips spreading on mine. "What's your surprise?" he asked as he pulled away from me, and I felt the longing in his breaths.

I didn't answer him with my words. My fingers crept between us to grip the hem of my shirt and lift it off. His mouth left me to go for my bare breasts, and I dropped back my head as he teased my nipples with his tongue. I saw a tiny sliver of light from beneath my mask, and I longed to see him. I reached toward my mask, but he caught it and stopped my ascent.

"If you don't follow this one rule, sweet girl, then we can't play. You can't remove that mask. Do you understand?" His voice was sharp and unexpected. I nodded and dropped my hand. "Don't worry about what I look like and just worry about me fucking your pussy with my tongue."

"Guy," I moaned as his kisses trailed down my bare stomach.

His hands raced up my thighs, and he lifted my skirt, bunching it at my waist. "No panties? Good girl," he praised before his tongue found the space between my legs.

I gripped his thick, wavy hair to balance myself as he lifted one of my legs to spread me for him. I moaned as his tongue slipped through my wet slit and traveled back to the entrance. He sank his tongue into me, each flick directed right at my most sensitive spot. Everything was amplified by my loss of sight. His electric touch coursed through me with every swipe of his tongue. I gasped as he bit my inner thigh and dragged his fingers through the wet mess he'd drawn from me.

"I want you to sit on my face," he said, and I choked on my own spit. I'd never done something like that.

"G-guy... no," I stammered. My self-consciousness soar to the front of my mind. I was frozen.

Mason

Sweet Harley was always insecure when she never needed to be. In the fleeting moments when I let myself forget she was my stepsister, her looks taunted me.

"What are you afraid of?" I asked.

"I just... I don't know." She choked on her words.

I smirked even though she couldn't see it. "Let me make you feel good."

Her head shook, and her hands reached for her skirt. "I don't think I'd like it."

I grabbed her wrists to stop her from covering herself. "Give me a chance to change your mind."

She nodded, a soft motion that still made her seem so unsure. The flush in her cheeks crept down her perfect chest. The guilt of seeing her naked—seeing her forbidden pussy—had waned. Instead of feeling guilty, I was selfish. I wanted all of her. Every bit of her. But I couldn't have her eyes, and that stung.

I guided her toward my bed and lay on my back as I

tugged her over my lap. I unzipped my pants and pulled out my cock so I could feel her against me for a moment before I brought her up to my mouth. Her warm wetness teased me, and I fought the urge to push inside her. She looked so nervous, her body tense and anxious, as she straddled my lap. I toyed with her nipples, caressing the flesh of her breasts until her breaths evened.

"Come up here," I said as I gripped her skirt and used it to drag her toward me.

Her hands gripped the headboard as her thighs fell to either side of my head. She smelled like nervous excitement, and her skin was sticky with sweat as I kissed the insides of her legs. Her breath hitched as I gripped her hips, much too roughly, and forced her down on my face. I wanted to be buried inside her. I wanted my face coated in her come.

I tongued her in a way I knew she'd never felt because her body reacted to every lap of my tongue as if it had given her a little shock. She was so sensitive when I curled my tongue along her swollen clit, making her whimper and squeeze the headboard harder.

"Guy," she forced out the word, sounding so small and unsure.

"Let go, sweet girl. Just relax and sit on my face." My grip tightened. "You won't be as sensitive if you just lower yourself right onto my tongue."

She dropped her weight into my grasp. She stopped jolting as I gave her long strokes with my tongue. Her protests turned to moans as her hips bucked against my mouth. I fucking ached as her muscles tightened beside my head, and she squeezed the metal headboard with all her might as she grinded on my face.

"Guy." She said my name again, but it had lost the hint of worry. Now it dripped with pleasure. Her body coursed with waves of it as she rode my face and coated my mouth and chin. "I'm going to come," she whispered as she tensed and moaned much too loud for a damn apartment, but I wasn't going to stop her ascent.

I gripped her hips and tugged her deeper into me, and she came on my face. I didn't let her hips go, giving her shallow strokes and making her twitch above me. She panted as she leaned over the metal and tried to still her trembling thighs.

I dragged her down my body, and her chest heaved against mine as she laid herself on top of me. I grabbed her chin and lifted her face to mine. "You can't see it, but your come is all over my fucking face. Taste yourself." I pulled her mouth to mine, then kissed her.

She whimpered against my lips as I spread them on hers. I wanted her to suck my cock, wanted to feel her warm mouth on me, but having her come on my face had me aching so intensely that I worried I'd come before I could feel her pussy again.

I rubbed my cock against her sensitive clit as she kissed me. I lifted my hips and pushed inside her. She was so warm and wet. She felt incredible. "My god, Hal—Harley." I corrected myself and hoped she didn't notice.

She didn't seem to as she dropped her head to my chest. I guided her with my grasp on her hips, her thighs still trembling with the residual effects of her orgasm. She gasped every time I pulled out, leaving just my tip inside her and letting my piercing tease her. The twitches of sensitivity from deep inside her brought me so damn close, and I hated that I couldn't last longer with her. She just excited me so much. I grabbed her hips and stayed buried for a moment as I tried to talk myself down in my head so I could keep fucking her.

"Remember when I said I had a surprise?" she said as she nuzzled into me.

"Yes," I said through clenched teeth.

"You don't have to pull out," she whispered, and a come-worthy smirk crossed her face. I didn't even know how I kept from busting right then at the thought of filling her up.

God, I didn't think this through.

It was so real. It was too far if I did that. It was riskier. It would be even more unforgivable if she found out. But fuck if those thoughts didn't get thrown away by my need to claim her pussy as mine and only mine.

I pulled out, rolled her onto her back, and crawled between her legs. I wished she wasn't wearing a blindfold, that I was the masked one so she could see just how much she pleased me when I came inside her. Just how good it felt to unleash within her.

"Are you sure, sweet girl?" I asked as I wrapped my hand behind her neck and tugged her up to my mouth. "You need to be really fucking sure." I rested my cock against her pussy.

"I'm sure. I want you to come inside me," she whimpered.

"You are such a good girl."

I growled as I kissed her. I drew back my hips and pushed inside her again, and just the thought of filling her brought me toward the edge as soon as I reached her depths. I dropped my face into the crook of her neck as I fucked her, hard and fast, until I came inside her. It felt... incredible.

She clenched and tightened around me as I filled her. It was uninhibited and wrong—so fucking wrong—but I didn't want to stop. I'd give up anything to be able to keep fucking her. Including my identity.

CHAPTER 17

Harley

I tucked my legs beneath me on the couch and typed out a text to Guy.

> What are you doing?

> Just getting in the shower. Wish I could have dragged you into one last night. Sorry I had to clean you up the best I could with just my tongue ;)

My cheeks flushed hot. Guy wouldn't give an inch about letting me see his face last night, even when I begged for a shower with him after being covered in our come. He wouldn't risk me seeing his face and wanting to leave him. I would never. I didn't care what he looked like. It wouldn't change how I felt about him or how my stomach fluttered when I talked to him. Well, he made more than my stomach flutter, but that was beside the point. I actually enjoyed his company. He was a good person, and that was all that mattered to me. He made me feel too good to ever think any less of him.

I smirked as I looked down at the screen and decided to make him wish he'd let us shower together. I looked around, climbed off the couch, and went to the bathroom.

I opened the door and got an eyeful. I didn't realize Mason was home, and I threw my hands over my eyes as if closing them was just not enough.

"Jesus Christ, Harley!" he yelled. He grabbed a towel in a rough motion that nearly knocked the bar loose.

"I'm sorry! I didn't know you were home!"

Behind my closed eyelids, something was etched into my mind's eye: Mason's dick in the mirror as he stroked it, a black bar under the head. My mouth dropped open.

The piercing.

The cut in his hand.

Oh god. Oh. My. Fucking. God. I backed away from the bathroom, my breath quickening with every step.

"No . . . no . . . n—" I repeated until his hands grasped my arms and stopped me.

Mason

JESUS FUCK. I ALWAYS LOCKED THE DOOR, BUT I WAS SO preoccupied with texting her that I'd forgotten. I didn't even think about anything aside from her maybe seeing my dick for a millisecond before her hands flew up to her face. But when she started panicking, backing out, and repeating the word *no*, I knew she knew. Harley was smart. She was so fucking smart. This was all too fucking stupid.

I shook her enough to get her to stop saying that damn word. "Yes!" I interrupted. "Yes, what you're thinking is right. And I'm sorry!"

Her hands lowered from her eyes, and her face reddened as she tried to stop the anger that was about to explode from her. "Sorry?" she hissed. "You're fucking *sorry*? For what? For sleeping with me?"

I shook my head. "I would never apologize for sleeping with you. Because I'm not sorry for that. I'm sorry I didn't tell you the truth."

Her mouth gaped. "Oh god, Mason . . ." Her anger transformed into this uncomfortable shock that made me uneasy. "I slept with you," she whispered, almost in a trance, as if she was locked in the memory of every night we'd been together. "Disgusting. Vile." The words seeped from her lips as the shock burned with renewed anger. "Piece of *shit*!"

"Hal," I said, dodging her biting words. "It was never meant to happen. But I'm not going to deny that it did, or that I wouldn't do it again. You actually liked me when I wasn't the monster you conjured up in your mind."

Her cheeks flamed red. "You sick son of a bitch." She reached for her phone and started to touch the screen. I grabbed it and looked at who she was calling. Her dad. I threw it to the floor, and it thudded on the carpet.

"Are you really calling your daddy, Harley? What are you going to tell him? That I forced myself on you? Or would you tell him that you came on my dick and all over my face?" The old Mason came out, the one who bullied her. I was being unfair. But I didn't care.

I heard her father's voice coming from the floor, saying a casual hello. I tightened my lips, picked up the phone, and shoved it in her face. "Go ahead, tell him," I whispered.

When she just stared at me, I repeated myself and pushed the phone into her trembling hand. "Tell him."

She shook her head and brought the phone up to her ear, tears forming at the corners of her eyes. "Sorry, Dad, I called you by mistake," she said with a hint of a waver in her voice. "Love you too, bye." She hung up the phone, her eyes never leaving mine. "Fuck you!" she said. "Get the hell out of my house!"

"Harley—"

"Get out!"

I didn't want to do it, but I backed away, went to my room and changed, and left like she asked. When I slammed the door behind me, it felt final, and I couldn't handle that. Once I had her, she was mine. She was mine whether I was Guy or Mason. Whether she was my stepsister or not.

Mine.

But I had no idea how she'd ever forgive me. She hated Mason, and she would never accept that she'd let me inside her.

I walked to my car, got inside, and drove back toward my apartment. When I pulled into the parking lot and walked up to my landing, I remembered how she'd blindfolded herself right outside my door just last night. When I went inside, my mind raced as I recalled kissing her against the wall and stripping her bare. In the bedroom, I remembered how she felt. How she tasted. Fuck. The reminders were nauseating. Stomach twisting. Heartbreaking. Having her love me felt worse than when she hated me. At least when she hated me, I didn't know what her moans sounded like.

CHAPTER 18

Harley

It had been over twenty-four hours since the last text from Guy—I mean, *Mason*—and even though I hated him for what he'd done, I missed our conversations. I missed learning about him.

I shivered. I had given Mason little chance to teach me anything about himself over the years. When I was talking to Guy, was I actually getting to know the true Mason? Or was it all just a part of his big, disgusting plan? Either way, I felt dirty. I was sickened by the idea of him inside me. He was family, even if we were estranged.

I looked at my phone and stared at the blank screen. It was hard to rationalize what had happened. It was almost too hard to even acknowledge. I was sick to my stomach over the entire ordeal, not just because he slept with me while using a fake identity, but because he made me fall for him. He was gross. He was worse than I ever imagined.

The doorbell rang, and I peeled away from my half-assed attempt to study. It was impossible to keep my mind on my finals when I was so stuck on Mason.

Someone stood outside my door, their hoodie up as they faced away from me. I couldn't tell who it was, but I opened the door because the pizza delivery guys often mistook this house for the one across the street. It happened at least once a week.

"Hey, you probably meant to stop at—"

The man turned around. There was no pizza in his hand. Even though it'd been years since I'd seen him face to face, I knew who he was. My words choked off in my throat at the sight of him.

"Nope, this is the right house." He pushed me inside and threw me against the wall. "Harley, Mason's sweet little sister," Jeff said in my ear. I shivered as his warm breath hit my skin.

I raised my chin with a feigned confidence. "Jeff, I have nothing to do with Mason."

"Oh, I know. I know a lot of things about you. What you like to drink. How you dance. But you and your little mystery man kept me from what I really wanted to know. How you *feel*." He laughed.

His words punched me in the gut and made me choke on my own spit. Mystery man? Mason? I had no time to straighten out the information he'd just given me. It just absorbed into me like a curse infiltrating my bloodstream. Mason was trying to protect me. In the only fucked-up way that he could, he was just trying to save me from Jeff. But it didn't make me feel any better, even if I wished it would have.

The door opened. Something heavy and plastic clattered to the ground, but I couldn't see past Jeff's head. He was ripped away from me and tossed to the floor.

"I told you to leave her alone!" Mason snarled as he drew his arm back and punched Jeff in the face. He hit him over and over again. I grabbed his arm, trying to stop him, but he just switched which hand he hit him with.

"Mason!" I screamed. "You're going to kill him!" Jeff was becoming a mangled mess beneath him. Blood saturated the tiled floors, splattering in dark contrast against the white.

Mason's gaze shot to me. "Did he touch you?" he asked, holding back his swing as he waited for my answer.

I shook my head, but I knew if Mason hadn't shown up, he would have. I would have been retribution for Mason's confession. Everything he'd told me was true.

Mason lowered his fist and shook out his hand. "Call the police," he said.

I fumbled with my phone, my fingers shaking too much to even dial those three numbers. I finally got it and gave them the address to my house.

When Mason clambered off Jeff, his arm was bleeding as if he'd been cut. "You're hurt," I said as I touched his bloody skin.

"Yeah, from that," Mason said as he motioned to the door.

I was so focused on keeping Mason from killing Jeff that I'd failed to notice what had made a sound when it had been dropped by the door. It was a cat carrier. Sammy meowed at me when I bent down and picked it up.

My eyes snapped to Mason. "Wh-why?"

"Because I knew you'd need him," he said as he washed his hands in the sink. He scrubbed his arm. "Like mother, like son. He's not a fan of me either."

"Aren't you allergic?" I asked.

He shrugged. "Yeah, my eyes are burning like hell." He

leaned over and splashed his face with cold water. He dried off and walked over to me, and the ice in his presence made me shiver. "And this is why I'm more of a dog person," he said with a curl of his lip as he pointed toward Sammy, who hissed at the gesture.

"You went home just to get him? For me?" I opened the carrier and tugged Sammy into me, burying my face in his orange coat. He started purring the moment I grabbed him.

He brought my cat to me. I was stuck on that, despite everything else that'd happened.

Mason

"Thank you, officers," I said as they turned to leave.

One looked back at me. "Are you sure you don't want to get checked out?"

"My hands will be fine."

The officer threw me a tight smile. "We'll be in touch about the rest of the report."

I nodded and followed them, to close the door once they'd left. Harley was just planted on the couch, petting that damn cat. I hated the thing, but if it wasn't for that cat, I wouldn't have found Harley and Jeff when I did. Before he could make good on his threat.

Without saying anything, I grabbed the cleaner under the sink and wiped the blood off the floor. I dropped the red-tinged paper towels in the garbage and washed my hands. The scent of bleach lingered on my skin as I dried them.

I walked to the front door and grabbed the handle, but

then I remembered what was burning a hole in my pocket. I reached inside and fondled the chain. With a deep breath, I went over to Harley and threw the contents of my pocket into her lap. Sammy hissed and ran off. She grabbed it and picked it up, looking at it in the palm of her hand. Her eyes welled with tears.

"Happy eighteenth birthday, Hal," I said as I turned to walk away.

"Mason," she whispered, but I refused to turn back. I had to go. "Will you put it on me?" She raised her voice at the end, trying to get me to stop.

It worked. I wiped a hand through my hair and turned back toward her. "Stand up," I said as I motioned her up.

She turned away from me and lifted her hair. I grabbed both ends of the chain and hooked them together. When she turned back toward me, I sucked in a breath. Those evergreens that I hated had never looked prettier.

My heartbeat quickened, and I knew I had to leave. I urged myself out. *Leave. I need to leave.* My legs betrayed me and kept me planted in front of her. "Why aren't you scared of me anymore, Harley?" I asked. "Is it because it took *all* that to finally get you to believe that I'm not some horrible monster?" I wanted her to push me away because I couldn't do it myself. I backed her into the glass overlooking the pool in the backyard. "Or am I the monster you always thought I was, one who would deceive you like I did, but you just got brave?"

"Mason," she whispered. The word made me shiver, and it couldn't. What we had couldn't happen. It had to end.

"Don't, Harley."

"You can't just leave," she said as her gaze rolled up to mine.

"I sure as fuck can, and I will. You were just a challenge,

that's it. Nothing more. So leave it at that," I lied, though the anger in my words was real. I was just angry for different reasons.

"You don't mean that."

"What do you think this can be, Hal?" I raised my voice. "I'm your brother. I grew up beside you. It's wrong, and I knew it was wrong, and I still did it. But it has to stop here. It can't be anything. *We* can't be anything. Let Guy live in your memory and forget about me."

A tear fell down her cheek, and she wiped it away and tried not to waver. In her heart she knew I was right. She had to. Because we were *very* wrong.

"No."

"God damn it, Harley! I took advantage of you. I *used* you. I was selfish with your body. I'm everything you've always said I am." My hand rose to her throat, and she gasped as I leaned into her and inhaled her scent for the last time. "I'm just glad, for once in your entire life, you took the time to get to know the real me." One of her tears slid past her jaw and hit my hand, and I fought all temptation to wipe it away.

She reached up and gripped my wrist, not to tug it away, but to hold me there. "You said you'd tell me a poem," she said, blinking her eyes to try to push her tears away.

I laughed. After all I'd just said, that was all she could say? Something about a stupid fucking poem? "What if that was a lie too?"

"It wasn't," she whispered as her lower lip trembled.

I rubbed a hand down my chin. "Temptation is rarely good, especially when it's forbidden. She's the fruit. Nothing will keep me from biting into her." I lifted my hand from her neck and ran my thumb along her lower lip. "Even if she didn't lick herself from my chin, we'd both still be banished." My hand snaked behind her and fisted her hair, lifting her chin toward me. "Paradise wasn't the place we left. It was with *her*." The last word came out low and seductive, because that was how I felt when I wrote it. Like she was paradise. Even as I tried to force myself to feel different, it was true. Her breath hitched as I leaned closer to her mouth. "You're my forbidden fruit, sweet girl," I whispered, nearly touching her lips. "I'm trying so hard not to take another bite of you."

CHAPTER 19

Harley

Sweet girl. That nickname made me melt. I looked up into his intense eyes, and they darkened with the same temptation he'd written about. I grabbed the back of his neck and tugged him into me. He kissed me back.

"You've never seen how I look when I see you naked." He pulled away to whisper.

I shook my head. His hands gripped the hem of my shirt and lifted it off. He took a step back and stared at me, and insecurity wrapped around me. It was hard to have his eyes on me when I could see his face. When I could see how he bit his lower lip as he stared at me and slowly rolled his gaze down to my chest. Heat crept across my face.

"So damn sexy, but still so wrong, sweet girl." His hand grazed my chest and gripped the flesh of my breast, then slid farther down and slipped beneath the waistband of my leggings. A growl vibrated in his throat as he leaned into me and devoured my mouth. He gripped the front of my pants with a frustrated exhale.

His forehead dropped to mine. "Damn it, you are sinful, Hal. Everything in my head tells me to stop. But my heart wants more."

"Take more," I whispered as I gripped his wrist and pushed his hand lower.

"Do you know what you're asking?"

I nodded.

"Do you really, though?" His hand spread and he palmed me, and I inhaled a sharp breath. "You're asking for me—for all intents and purposes, your brother—to fuck you again. That's so fucked up," he said with a smirk against my mouth. "How could you still want me inside you?"

I responded with the buck of my hips against his hand.

He tugged off his shirt and that familiar body now looked foreign to me. I ran a hand down the curves of his chest and stomach. When I closed my eyes, everything felt native. His warm hand on me, his hardness against my hip, the way each breath left his mouth in that same hungry way they always had behind that mask. His low, seductive voice reminded me of every syllable he'd ever spoken to me as Guy. My body responded to those memories as I tilted my pelvis and grinded against his hand.

"Good girl, Hal," he whispered as he dropped his lips to my neck and kissed me. Mason's nickname for me didn't stop the motion of my hips, and soon, they stopped being two different people entirely. I moaned as I dropped back my head and bathed in his familiar touch. His fingers spoke to me in my native language as they slipped inside me.

"Mason, I need you," I panted.

He lifted his head and his dark eyes intensified. "I love when you call me that," he growled.

"It's just your name," I whispered.

"It's not just the name. It's the way you say it. Without

the hatred you've had for the last decade. It sounds different, wrapped in your pleasure."

Mason

OH, GOD. THE WAY SHE SAID MY NAME AND BATHED IT IN THE moans on her tongue . . . Fuck. It was the most beautiful sound I'd ever heard. I throbbed and ached for her. I couldn't wait a single moment longer to feel her around me again. Not as Guy, not hidden behind a mask, but as me. The man of her dreams and nightmares.

I turned her around and put her hands in front of her. Her breath fogged the glass, which had cooled from the descending fall temperature. My hand moved down her chest, through the valley of her breasts, and tugged down her leggings. My fingertips sought the heat of her ass, and I gripped the warm flesh.

"Say my name, sweet girl. Beg for me," I growled.

"Mason," she panted, "please."

I leaned into her and lifted her chin, turning her just enough so I could look at those gray eyes that once haunted me but now soothed me. "Please what, Hal?"

"Fuck me," she moaned with a frustrated wiggle of her hips against me.

"Why? Tell me why you want me." I tightened my grip on her chin.

Her lower lip trembled, as if I was forcing her to confront what I knew was inside her. What she would struggle to admit. But I wanted to hear it come from her parted lips. I wanted her to say it to me.

"Because I love you, Mason," she whimpered.

I rubbed my hand down the curve of her neck. "In all the years I've known you, you've never said those words to me."

"I didn't know you."

"You suddenly know me now because I've made you come?" I asked.

She shook her head. "No, because I wouldn't let myself get to know you."

I rubbed my cock against her slit. "Do you like what you learned about me?"

She nodded, biting her lower lip.

I pushed inside her, and it felt different from any other time. It felt free, not just because my bare cock was inside her, but because it was *my* bare cock instead of Guy's. Because she was *mine*, not Guy's.

She whimpered as I sank into her, but it wasn't enough. The moans she breathed against the glass weren't enough. I pulled out of her, turned her around, and let her kick off her discarded leggings. I lifted her thigh and spread her legs. Looking into her face was euphoric. Seeing those gray eyes staring at me, the real me, was better than any orgasm I'd had. I could only imagine how cataclysmic it would feel when I filled her this time.

I eased inside her, my piercing catching on her for a moment before I pushed past and stretched her around me. I wrapped my hand around the back of her neck and drew her into me as my other hand reached for her chest, toying with her nipple in the way I knew she loved. When I kissed her, her lips met mine with a hunger that rivaled my own.

I leaned into her neck, growling against her flesh. "I love you, sweet girl. I shouldn't, but I do. I never thought I was capable of loving another person, but you live in my mind all the time, Hal. All the time. I'd do anything to have you and keep you safe, and if that isn't love, I don't know what is."

Tears welled in her eyes. "How do I know?" she asked.

I thrust hard and deep into her and moved my hand from her breast to her cheek. "Because I'd have left you if you'd wanted me to. I'd have let you go because your happiness means more than . . . anything. I brought you your damn cat because I didn't want you to deal with a breakup alone, even if it was over me." My eyes still burned like the fiery depths of hell because that cat was all over her face and lap, everywhere that I wanted to touch her. But it didn't matter. I'd deal with the burn if it meant being able to be with her. I'd deal with the little orange asshole to be with her. I'd do anything for her, and I wasn't exaggerating.

She buried her face into my neck, and I stalled my thrusts to bathe in her affection. Lived in the moment of her soft posture, rigid only from pleasure and not from harbored anger. Enjoyed our faces pressed together as her forehead met mine with nothing between us.

I couldn't last with her. If I had known I would be inside her again, that she'd let me fuck her, I'd have better prepared myself. I pulled out of her and gripped the base of my dick, talking down my pleasure.

I dragged her to the couch and sat her down, falling to my knees between her legs. My hands hooked around her thighs as I tugged her to the edge of the couch and buried my face in her wet warmth. She tasted so fucking good, even better when I could look up and see those eyes staring back at me. Her hands gripped my hair as I ate her like she was the only thing that would satiate this hunger. Long strokes with my tongue left her trembling. I didn't stop until she came on my face, until her moans erupted from her in the most beautiful song I'd ever heard. Even once her trembling body jolted with the aftershocks of her orgasm, I still licked at her come, cleaning her up so I could dirty her all over again.

I offered her the devilish smirk that got her even when she hated me. When I rose to my feet and sat beside her, it was too easy to bring her spent body onto my lap. She melted into me as her wet pussy rubbed along the length of my aching dick. Fuck, I needed her. I'd never needed anything more.

I reached between us and put myself inside her. She gasped. I gripped her hips roughly and raised mine to meet hers, a groan leaving my lips as her twitching walls squeezed me. I used my grip on her hips to move her on my lap as I got too close, wanting to keep myself buried inside her.

"I'm going to come," I groaned. "Fill you up again because you're mine. Are you my sweet girl?"

She whimpered and nodded. "Yes, Mason. I'm yours."

"Good girl," I growled against her lips as I kissed her. As much as she was mine, I was hers. I had made a lot of mistakes in my life, but I wanted her to be the last.

My last mistake.

EPILOGUE

Mason

"Mason, you're in a good mood," my mother said as she pulled the pan from the oven. I didn't notice that I was in any particular mood, but okay. Unless she meant the quiet between Harley and me. Usually we'd take shots at each other, accompanied by enough eye rolls to last till the next holiday dinner.

"It's been a while since I've been here, that's all. On my best behavior," I said as I grabbed plates from the cabinet. My eyes roved down Harley's body as I set the table. I stared at the dark makeup encasing her grey eyes and the black wings of long eyelashes exploding off them. My eyes drifted downward to her cut college hoodie, the thick fabric falling off her right shoulder. I knew what was beneath those letters across her chest.

"Excuse me," she said as she reached past me and placed the silverware onto the table.

I coughed as my mother came up behind me, and I tried

to hide my erection that was pressing against the family dinner table.

Dinner was served, and I sat as far away from Harley as I could, like I would have before I'd fucked her. I kept watching her mouth with every bite she took. The way her lips wrapped around her fork, she knew what she was doing.

"You two are so quiet," her father said.

"What is there to say?" she said with a shrug of her shoulder.

I smirked. "You could tell them about how you failed that math class," I said.

Her father lowered his glass with a heavy sigh. "Really, Harley?"

She swirled her finger around her own glass and nodded, but not before she shot me a dagger-filled look.

"At least I didn't get fired from my job," she bit back. Her attitude went right to my dick.

I tightened my smile. "I didn't get fired. I quit before they could fire me, thank you very much."

"Smart move," she said with a sarcastic sway of her head.

"Thanks. And I didn't even need an expensive college degree to learn it."

We poked at each other just like we had while growing up. Our parents seemed to relax once we started arguing, probably because the silence between us had been strange. We needed things to seem normal.

Last Mistake

Harley

"Shh," he said as he pushed me into his bedroom. Mason looked around before he closed the door. "You're going to get us in trouble," he scolded as I tried to control my giggling. I could hardly get through dinner with a straight face. His mouth found mine, and I kissed him back, but then I stopped him.

"We can't do what you're thinking about doing," I said as I gestured toward his hard cock against my lower belly.

"I've been thinking about that since you walked in the door, Hal," he said, his voice low. "I was thinking about how much I'd love to shut your sassy mouth up with this." He gripped my hand and brought it to the front of his jeans, rubbing me against him. "You didn't need to tell them about my job," he said through a groan.

"You didn't need to tell them about my failed class either. Besides, they're used to your failures, not mine," I said with a smirk as I leaned closer to his mouth.

"Ouch. If I wasn't so fucking horny for you, that might have hurt my feelings."

There was no lock on Mason's door, and I weighed out the risk as he gripped my shoulders and urged me down on my knees. I looked up at him as he undid his jeans and pulled out his cock. After a final glance at the door, I threw caution to the wind and took him into my mouth.

He growled, a deep throaty sound that made me throb. It was bad enough we were stepsiblings, but we took it to a whole different level when we started playing around with our parents in the same house. When I looked up at him, he clearly couldn't care less as he gripped the back of my head and pushed his cock farther into my mouth.

"Good girl," he groaned as my tongue worked his

piercing in the way I knew he liked. He shook his head and tugged me off his dick. "I need your pussy, sweet girl," he said as he helped me to my feet.

His hot hand rubbed my exposed shoulder. He laid me down on the bed, and my breath hitched the moment he climbed over me. I remembered my friend beneath him, in the same exact position. I shook my head and forced my focus back to Mason as his hands gripped the waistband of my leggings and tugged them down my thighs. He slipped them off and crawled over me to kiss me.

"Mason," I whispered as his hands gripped my face in a comforting grasp.

"Are you thinking about Anna right now?" he asked.

He knew me; he always knew what was going through my mind. Ever since we were little. But instead of exploiting my pain until I was left a sobbing mess, he now comforted me.

"Don't think about anyone but me," he whispered as he leaned down and caught my attention with his mouth. "Pretend there wasn't anyone else before you, because I wasn't the person I am now. With you. Because of you."

I exhaled against his lips and kissed him back.

He didn't make a move toward his cock until I relaxed beneath him. Once I did, his hand slipped down, and he pushed inside me. I moaned as he stretched me and his piercing raked my skin like it always did. My sounds grew as his thrusts went deeper, and he shoved a hand over my mouth.

In the silence, with his hips stalled, I heard my father's voice. He was talking on the phone, not far from the door. My cheeks flushed, and my skin crawled with heat at the thought of getting caught beneath Mason. I tried to push him away, my eyes widening as he remained steadfast and immovable.

He leaned down and whispered in my ear. "I don't want to stop. Keep quiet, sweet girl." He pulled his hand away from my mouth and let me pant out my panic.

"Mason, are you out of your mind?" I asked as his hand snaked around the back of my neck and tugged me into him.

"A little," he whispered, and his signature smirk melted some of my fear. "I kinda like the idea of fucking Daddy's little girl when he's just outside that door."

"I'm not a daddy's girl," I whispered back as the pulse of his hips made me bite my tongue to keep from moaning.

I hated that he thought of me that way, but he was right that it was exciting me in ways it shouldn't. All of tonight excited me, actually. The way we subtly flirted in front of our parents. Doing such a naughty thing beneath their roof. All of it. It made me ache for an orgasm.

"Make me come, Mason," I said through a soft moan.

"You sure you can be quiet enough?" he asked as he curled his hips and slipped a hand between us.

I nodded, but I wasn't wholly confident that I could control my voice as he worked me with his hands the way he did. I came too loudly with him because he touched me in ways that I couldn't even explain. He touched me like he'd known me my whole life, and he pretty much had.

He stroked my clit, and I put my hand over my mouth to control the brewing scream. My whimpers were still too loud.

"You aren't going to be quiet enough," he whispered, stopping his fingers' movements between my legs. I still heard my father's voice as he talked on the phone.

Mason put his weight onto me and put his hand over my

hand, silencing me except for the heavy breathing from my nose. He started rubbing me again and didn't stop until I was arching my back in pleasure.

"Come for me, sweet girl," he growled as he fucked me harder, the bed frame rattling as he rubbed between my legs.

I came, panting as he drew his hand away and thrust until he came inside me. He hardly kept his own moans quiet as his hips stuttered against me. He kissed me, his cock still twitching. He pulled out of me and zipped up his jeans. He helped me to my feet and handed my leggings to me.

"I need to clean up," I told him as I tried to look for something to use. He grabbed my hands and rubbed my palms.

"I want you to sit through dessert while filled with my come." His words made me shiver. "And I'll wear you for the rest of tonight." He rubbed up the front of his pants. "I love you," he whispered as he kissed me. "Now go pretend to hate me as my come drips from you."

This ebook originated as a serial romance on Patreon, where Lauren's reader-driven stories are shared weekly. Join to be a part of Spicy Story Sundays! www.patreon.com/LaurenBielAuthor

CONNECT WITH LAUREN

Check out LaurenBiel.com to sign up for the newsletter and get VIP (free and first) access to Lauren's spicy novellas and other bonus content!

Join the group on Facebook to connect with other fans and to discuss the books with the author. Visit http://www.facebook.com/groups/laurenbieltraumances for more!

Lauren is on Patreon! Get access to even more content and sneak peeks at upcoming novels. Check it out at www.patreon.com/LaurenBielAuthor to learn more!

ACKNOWLEDGMENTS

Thank you to all my patrons who have helped make this story and others possible.

Thank you to my editors for helping make this story the best it could be.

Husband, I love you. Now put a mask on for me!

ALSO BY LAUREN BIEL

To view Lauren Biel's complete list of books, visit:

www.LaurenBiel.com

Or

Campsite.bio/LaurenBielAuthor

ABOUT THE AUTHOR

Lauren Biel is the author of many dark romance books, with several more titles in the works. When she's not working, she's writing. When she's not writing, she's spending time with her husband, her friends, or her pets. You might also find her on a horseback trail ride or sitting beside a waterfall in Upstate New York. When reading her work, expect the unexpected. To be the first to know about her upcoming titles, please visit www.LaurenBiel.com.

Made in the USA
Middletown, DE
06 November 2023